Cypress Grove

Cypress Grove

Rose Boucheron

PIATKUS

All the charac　　　　　　　　　　　　　　　　　　al persons,

Judy Piatkus (Publishers) Ltd of
5 Windmill Street, London W1T 2JA
email: info@piatkus.co.uk

Chapter One

The village of Cypress Grove sat in the Cotswolds; it was not perhaps as well known or popular as the other famous villages, but nevertheless it had a charm all its own. With its old church, St Rupert's, and the cypress grove leading up to it, it mainly consisted of a village green with small lanes leading off.

It was famous for its hotel, The Old Manor House, which had originally been a stately home owned by the Barrington family. It had a High Street and side turnings, lots of little shops, mainly owned by the families who had held them for many years.

Sometimes people driving about the Cotswolds came upon the village as a surprise; for it had none of the ambience of Burford or Stow-on-the-Wold or Bourton-on-the-Water. Its one claim to fame was the hotel, a prestigious, luxury hotel, known throughout the country as a haven of good living, which kept up standards that people with money expected.

The village was a hotchpotch of dwellings – shops, cottages, Georgian homes, and the village green, triangular in shape, at one end of which stood the church. It was small inside, but with wonderful stained-glass windows, and was well patronised by the locals.

There was small building given over to council matters; a brass plate outside said COUNCIL OFFICES but this was a misnomer. For although some council work did go on there, more important matters were referred to the nearest town. At the moment the council was discussing, or arguing, about the merits of a shop to be opened as a Thai restaurant; no one was in favour of this, except the man who had put in the application, whose address had been Shepherd's Bush. They already had an Italian restaurant, and that had taken enough discussion, but now it was here, and it was well patronised. For an expensive evening there was the hotel and a small restaurant called The Yellow Duck, for no apparent reason, since there was not a village pond, or a decent pond in the area. For afternoon tea, there was Barbara's Pantry, which did serve the most wonderful teas, with scones that melted in the mouth, served with cream and raspberry or strawberry jam, and you could get a decent light lunch there.

The chemist was run by a Bruce MacDonald and his wife Anne, a Scots couple, who both wore white coats and took their jobs very seriously. He had a small moustache and looked like Charlie Chaplin. There was an off licence and a general stores incorporating the newsagents and much local gossip generated from there.

The one dress shop was run by a lady in her early forties, a Ms Genella Hastings, very elegant, who had the most wonderful dress displays, and visitors often found themselves drawn in and came out having bought. The locals thought she may have come from London or Oxford. She was reticent and seldom took part in local affairs. Genella Hastings was divorced, though it was believed she had a man friend who visited her. The word lover was not used. He had been seen going in and out of the side door in the evenings.

There was a small house for sale on the village green with a saleboard outside. The owner had recently died and his relatives were waiting for a decent price before they let it go. Ned Jenkins, who had owned the house, lived there alone after the death of his wife many years before. He had been in charge of the stables at Barrington Manor, the original manor house now long gone and it was reputed that one of the daughters of the house had been having an affair with him.

The family: it had been Mrs Ashby who owned it, she and her husband Denis Ashby having taken over her parents' legacy of the manor when they died, turning it into a top-quality hotel. The Ashbys had two grown-up daughters and two sons, and it had been the elder daughter, Marsha, who had fallen for the groom. The affair had created quite a scandal at the time and she had been sent away to France to stay with relatives, while Ned Jenkins had been given the cottage as a gift to keep him quiet when he left his employment. Locals passed the house as though it was a house of disrepute, and no one from the area thought of buying it.

The antiques-shop man, Mark Hazlitt, ran the shop on his own after his wife left him for a London dealer. It was full of exquisite things, all high-class antiques. Although one seldom saw people in there, he did quite a business. Clients from outlying districts came in to the village and he had a waiting list of people wanting special pieces or works of art.

Granny Holden lived in the tiny cottage at the end of Lamb Street, with her granddaughter Bernice, who was a receptionist at The Old Manor House.

There was quite a considerable number of staff at the hotel. The head waiter, called Anton although he wasn't French, was excellent at his job. His wife also worked in the hotel as a chambermaid. The chef, Hobis, was excellent – the most important man in the hotel and known throughout the world. The hotel needed to keep up its reputation as one of the finest small hotels in the country. But, now that his wife had died, Denis Ashby was finding it increasingly difficult to run.

The Old Manor House was busy all the year round, even in winter, and especially at Christmas. You could have a wonderful Christmas there but, of course, it would cost you, and it was surprising to the locals at least, how many people could afford to stay there. But it seemed to the country dwellers, the locals, that these days more and more people had so much money that spending it was no problem, while others, like some cottagers in the village, couldn't find a penny between them.

There was also a nursing home tucked away at the end of Lamb Street, the Cypress Nursing Home and local people hoped they would end their days there – that is, if it wasn't too expensive for their relatives to keep up the cost of care. It was run by a Mrs Marsden, who was nothing if not severe and her word was law. She did, though, have excellent helpers – both paid staff and voluntary workers.

One of the little shops had been empty for so long that application had been made to turn it into a charity shop. It was argued between the councillors that it would raise money for Oxfam or the Red Cross if the owner could be persuaded to allow them to take over the shop rent free. This he did, although he was known as a skinflint but at the first offer from a buyer, he said, it must close. The councillors urged that it should look tasteful from the outside and, as one of them (a retired Londoner) said, 'not like an old toot shop'.

The women of village were delighted and took turns to help out in it. They were not deluged with gifts but somehow it kept going. Mrs Turnbull ran it, having once worked in Marks and Spencer before her retirement and she was a dab hand at her job. They made it their business to dress the window attractively, bringing flowers from their gardens; there was never a shortage of women working there, although it was unpaid, except for Mrs Turnbull, who was paid for her job of manageress.

No one knew how far back the cypress tress had been planted, for they had grown tall and lanky, and the passage to the church was quite dark now. Many a love tryst was

4

held there; it had become a meeting place over the years. Women, now with families, often smiled as they went through the dark arcade, pushing a pram or holding the hand of a toddler.

The church was built in 1692 and this date was engraved into the stone over the entrance. In spring the churchyard was strewn with daffodils, but apart from relatives and friends bringing flowers to their departed loved ones, it was mainly set off by yew trees.

'What a dear little place!' visitors said as they left it. 'I'd like to come again. . .'

Chapter Two

At two o'clock in the morning, the city of Bath had never looked more beautiful. So thought Robert Markham, the manager of the hotel Beau Nash, as he stood at the window of his apartment on the top floor: the twinkling lights, the sheer position of the city in the West Country, to say nothing of its history and its architecture.

He moved away from the window and, taking off his evening jacket, removed his tie and eased his collar. Going into the bedroom, he saw that his wife, Grace, was fast asleep; he had sent her up soon after midnight, either that, or she would have kept going until four in the morning, checking, rechecking, which everyone knew was the secret of a well-run hotel.

And they had enough staff – from the bellboys, to the chambermaids, the restaurant staff, the excellent house-keeper Mrs Goode and her assistants, their exalted chef, Bodor, with his irascible temper, and his assistants. He had no complaints on that score.

He made his way to the bathroom and, looking in the mirror, saw not for the first time that he had aged in the six years since they had taken over the Beau Nash. He lifted his chin, yes, even his moustache, that clipped small moustache that he always wore, was sprinkled with grey, while his black hair was thinning now, that thick lustrous head of hair he had had when young.

Still, his teeth were good, he thought, brushing them, and he wasn't all that tired after an evening such as this had been.

A splendid evening, with dinner thrown in, dancing into the small hours, the speakers down from London from the Royal Society, American guests, yes, quite an evening, but then the Beau Nash was famous for its well-organised special evenings. But it kept the staff busy, they had to be on their toes twenty-four hours a day.

As he changed and got ready for bed, half his mind was on the item he had seen in the *Brewers' Weekly* that morning and he went into his study and retrieved the paper, sinking back on to his bed half dressed to study it.

Yes, there it was. A special item. The sale of a freehold, small luxury hotel in the Cotswolds. Privately owned, well, that would be a first, small, twelve bedrooms en suite, the usual facilities, a fabulous setting – it had apparently been a house of some distinction before being turned into an hotel some ten years before.

He leaned back, wide awake now. Recalling, remembering the small luxury hotel he and Grace had run before coming here. In the heart of Leicestershire, Quorn country, The Swan had been famed for its exclusivity, the luxury of the rooms and the service, and he and Grace had made sure it stayed that way.

They had been delighted when the brewers announced that they had secured the management of The Swan and had been loath to leave. They had been there eight years until the possibility of running the Beau Nash in Bath had come up. They had thought about it but not too long, knowing that it would be a feather in their caps if they could secure it, and probably their last chance to run such a large and prestigious hotel.

Well, it had been all worth while. And they had enjoyed every moment, hard work though it was. No one could pretend it was easy, but what an achievement! They were the perfect couple to run an hotel, this one probably one of

7

the finest in the country, and they were experienced, for they had looked after both loud and noisy pubs in London and seaside monstrosities. But they were both ambitious, and now, heaven knows they had worked hard enough.

This advertisement intrigued him – apart from anything else it was his and Grace's favourite place, the Cotswolds. And he wondered where it might be. He fell to thinking of the possibilities and that was how Grace found him, still on top of the bedclothes, still holding the newspaper, breathing quietly.

She eased the newspaper away and folded it and smiled down at him. It was six o'clock; she always woke at around this time being a creature of habit even on Sunday, which was often their day off. Tiptoeing into the bathroom, she smiled as she thought of the success of the evening before. No doubt about it, another triumph for the Beau Nash. But now she would make herself some tea.

Taking the tea back to bed, she picked up the paper idly, and soon her eye fell on the heavily lined advertisement. She stared out towards the window. Was this what he had been looking at? Whatever it was he had been engrossed; something had caught his eye. She too read the advertisement and began to ponder. Surely, surely he wasn't thinking, seriously thinking?

Sipping her tea, she glanced over at him, and saw that his eyes were open, and he was watching her, sleepily, blinking, but awaiting her reaction.

'You have to be joking!' she said, but she smiled.

He pulled the bedclothes over him. 'I'd like some tea,' was all he said.

'I'll get it,' she said, and felt more strongly than ever that he was serious about this. It had captured his imagination.

She brought back the tray and put it down in front of him.

'Now,' she said, 'out with it.'

He took the paper from her. 'Can't you see it, Grace?'

he said. 'Little country place, small, twelve rooms, possibly a private residence at one time, the Cotswolds. I wonder where it is?'

'But you've never mentioned the possibility of leaving the Beau before,' and she frowned. 'I thought we were good for a few more years yet.'

'But Grace, I am not saying that I am too old for it, nor you, of course, but the idea of going back to the country, it's very tempting, don't you think so?' He sipped his tea.

'Well,' she said slowly. 'I agree that at times it's a bit much but after a night like last night, it's all worth while.'

He glanced at the paper again. 'There is something about the advertisement, also the fact that it is freehold, now, we've never had that, always a tied house. We would be free, Grace, free to retire when we liked, we would own something – that's what appealed to me, apart from anything else. Something for the kids, the girls, the future.'

'I had no idea you felt like this,' she said. 'We're doing all right – our savings and investment, such as they are – girls all settled and off our hands.'

'Yes, but don't you see, we would be free, our own agents, and that's something we've never been – always answerable to someone else.'

'We've been spoiled,' she said. 'I've often thought how lucky we are, with no responsibilities.'

'Well, up to point,' he said, looking at her. 'Are you dead set against the idea?' he asked, his small brown eyes looking into hers. Almost pleadingly, she thought.

It wouldn't do any harm to humour him. Obviously he had this bee in his bonnet, and who was she to deny him something he wanted? He had been the best husband ever and she adored him. She could never refuse him anything he really wanted, even though this idea of moving again had been the last thing on her mind.

'Well, give them a ring later in the morning,' she said. 'As I say, I am not totally averse to the idea, although I am still surprised you are even considering it.'

He went off to shower and get changed and she picked up the advertisement again and reread it. Certainly it sounded tempting and, like Robert, she adored the Cotswolds. Their lifestyle at The Swan had suited them very well. Not too much pressure, lovely country area, and certainly the idea of owning something of their very own appealed to her.

When he returned from the bathroom she could feel the restrained excitement emanating from him like an aura.

'What shall we do today?' she asked him, to lower the tension. 'Go for a run? We could ring Molly and invite ourselves over for tea – see little Jake – how about that?'

'Great,' he said. Anything to take his mind off this Cotswolds thing.

'Don't mention—' he began.

'As if—'

They were in perfect harmony.

She left him to go downstairs with his bunch of keys to cheek the situation, hardly necessary for the Beau Nash was run on oiled wheels.

It was a fine morning as they set out for Chippenham, where their daughter Molly and her husband Peter ran a wine shop. Their ultimate aim was to run a small hotel like their parents, for the brewery was a closed world to outsiders and hotels and public houses were inclined to stick together.

They tended to go more often to Molly and Peter's, since she was the nearer of their three daughters and had given birth to their only grandson. Nothing they liked more than seeing this little chap, just two years old and like his grandpa.

It wasn't until they were on the way home that the Cotswold subject was mentioned again.

'You are serious about this project, aren't you?' Grace asked him as they neared Bath.

'Now, do I ever waste time on things that don't matter?' he asked.

She couldn't argue with that.

He parked the car in the hotel garage and they went up in the lift to the top floor.

Grace had pulled the blinds against the afternoon sun and now the evening sun flooded the room. She stood looking out for a few moments while Robert went downstairs to check all was well.

Yes, she would miss this fantastic city, the life they had, always on the go, but so rewarding. And the view from this window!

She reflected for a moment. They were both sixty and worked as hard as many half their age but they were used to it. Would a quieter life suit them now? Being on the go twenty-four hours a day kept them alert and fresh, she was sure. Were they ready for a bucolic life? Then she smiled to herself. Running an hotel, of any size, was hardly an easy life. And she had to admit to a slight curiosity about the wording of the advertisement.

Well, they would soon know.

When Robert returned, he brought two glasses on a tray, a whisky for himself and wine for Grace. He sat down beside her, looking out on to the glory that is Bath.

'Most beautiful city in the country,' he said.

'I'll go along with that,' Grace said and they sat until the evening sun went down.

She noticed that he didn't mention the advertisement again.

It was ten-thirty the next morning before they surfaced from their work downstairs. A coffee break, then a return to the busy world of the Beau Nash. And it was lunch time before she saw him again, and by then he had made his phone call.

He took a deep breath and got to work on the internet.

'Well, here it is,' he said, as he opened an e-mail. 'Shall I read it to you? It is in a village called Cypress Grove—'

'What? Where's that?'

11

'In Gloucestershire—'

'I know that, darling—'

'Well, some miles from Stow, Burford, Moreton, and it is called The Old Manor House.'

'How original,' Grace said.

He glanced at her. 'Look, if you are not interested, I may as well—'

'Oh, Robert dear, I'm sorry, I think I am a bit excited about it myself. It just sounds too good to be true.'

'It has twelve rooms, en suite, well, come and look at the picture.'

They stared at the photograph. 'Oh, Robert! It's lovely!'

There it sat: the entrance at the end of a circular drive through a lovely garden, a house built in Cotswold stone, the garden itself laid out with trees and flowers with a lichgate at the other end.

'It has a flat built on, for us, and an indoor swimming pool, also added at a later date, a large conservatory, an attic floor for staff.'

'They certainly went to town when they turned it into an hotel,' Grace said.

They sat absorbing it all for half an hour before Robert decided and told her his plans.

'Look, we can't both be away at the same time, so how about if I took half a day off on Thursday and if it comes up to expectation, we'll both go on Sunday? I'll leave early in the morning, around eight, and I should be back by soon after lunch.'

'What's on Thursday?' she asked, consulting her diary.

'Twenty-four to lunch – Fine Arts – those Americans off to see the quilts; in the evening several dinner parties, but I shall be back by then. Can you manage?'

'Can I manage!' she laughed.

When Thursday came round it was a fine May morning and Robert set off, taking the familiar road to the Cotswolds, and coming across quite a bit of early commuting traffic.

But the road soon became easier. He had to admit to a feeling of excitement as he got nearer to Cypress Grove and realised he had been through the village before but hadn't recognised the name.

A signpost directed him and he was on the village green. A triangular-shaped sward of grass, a church at the wide end with a pointed spire. A double row of cypress trees, possibly a path to the church, Robert thought. Houses and cottages surrounded it, all of Cotswold stone, with lots of steps and small windows. It was like coming home, Robert thought, reminded of The Swan. A narrow lane lay off to the right, Lamb Street, and an arrow pointing to The Old Manor House. His heart was beating with excitement as he approached slowly up the drive and round to the car park.

He sat back and took a deep breath, more impressed than he liked to admit. Was this house to be his future? He climbed out and locked the car, noticing the large tubs of tulips and the wisteria which climbed up on the side of the house to overhang the porch. Over the back entrance was a sign reading 1762 – was it really as old as that?

He pushed open the door and found himself in a flagged hall, at the end of which was the reception area. It was wide and welcoming and luxuriously furnished, with bowls of flowers and soft carpets and antique chairs. The two young women who were on duty gave him a warm smile.

'Good morning,' he said. 'My name is Markham, Robert Markham. I have an appointment with Mr Ashby.'

The girl smiled. 'He is expecting you,' she said, already pressing a bell on the counter.

'If you would like to take a seat,' she said, 'Mr Ashby will be with you directly.'

In no time, it seemed, Robert saw a tall, well-built man approaching. So this was Mr Ashby, the proprietor, and wondered if there was a Mrs Ashby.

Denis Ashby held out his hand in greeting – a warm smile and handshake and Robert was instantly reassured.

'How do you do?' he said 'Good journey?'

'Yes, fine, no problems,' Robert said.

'This way, we'll talk in my office.'

He led the way through to a room which might have been the library at some stage. Books still lined the walls and there were comfortable easy chairs. Robert already saw himself sitting there but on the other side of the desk.

Denis Ashby was a big man, Robert thought him to be in his late sixties or even seventy, but he carried himself well.

Ashby decided he liked this man. There was an air of integrity about him – and confidence. Dark brown eyes, that looked straight at you, an air of being in charge; he was alert, on the ball, not a man to be trifled with... Thus he summed Robert up in a matter of moments. He wasn't often wrong – he had studied human nature long enough in this present field.

'Well,' he said. 'You don't need me to tell you of the amount of interest I have had in this place and I will put my cards on the table. I know you have to get back so I won't beat about the bush. Before we begin, I have ordered coffee, it will be here in a moment,' and just then the door opened and a waiter came in with a tray of coffee.

After serving them, he sat back. 'This place, which was originally Barrington Manor, goes back quite a way. It belonged to my wife's family, but when her parents died we thought about it seriously and decided that we would try to get permission to turn it into a luxury hotel. We had no wish to continue living in it as a family home – we had four children – and opening it a weekends, that sort of thing, so we went about applying and looking into the idea of a luxury hotel. Well,' he smiled. 'It took us three years – planning permission, alterations, additions – that sort of thing. As it turned out, it was a great success, but you don't need me to tell you, because I know you've had plenty of experience in this field.'

Robert was fascinated. Without even looking over it, he knew he wanted it. Of course, the price was prohibitive and, if Ashby had such a lot of interest, he wasn't likely to be in the forefront of the applicants.

'May I ask why you are selling?' he said.

'My wife died,' Ashby said simply. 'A year ago.'

'I'm sorry.' The man must be devastated, Robert thought.

'And, I can't carry on on my own. So, hopefully I am going to live with my elder son in Portugal. We've been open ten years here so I've had a long run but I don't have to tell you it's hard work!'

He looked at Robert. 'Now that's my side of the story ... Are you still interested, would you like to see around?'

'Indeed I would,' Robert said. He could hardly wait.

Robert became more and more enamoured of the idea, the more he saw. The rooms had been decorated and furnished with great style, the kitchens were large and airy, he met the chef and some of the staff, saw the flat that he and Grace would live in, walked round the grounds, and the more he saw the more he wanted it. But the money...

Ashby offered him lunch, but he politely refused, explaining that he had to get back, but that he would like to bring Grace to see over it on Sunday.

Over a drink Ashby explained that he wanted to finance his son into buying such a hotel in Portugal. His other son was in South Africa. He was much impressed with Robert and Grace's history – he and his wife had come new to the business – and knew the setbacks.

'I must say,' he said. 'The Beau Nash in Bath – know it well. Stayed several times – but this of course is a different kettle of fish altogether but you don't need me to tell you that. I also,' he added, 'know The Swan. My wife and I stayed there once on our way up north. Excellent hotel.'

'Yes, I have very fond memories,' Robert said.

He couldn't wait to get back and tell Grace about it. He was a practical man, and knew that to get that excited about something was not always a good thing, but when he simmered down he knew he would temper it with common sense.

15

Besides – the money.

Grace awaited him with some trepidation but as soon as she saw his face could see the suppressed excitement.

She took his arm. 'Come and tell me all about it.'

They sat over a drink in the flat, while he talked to her about the whole project.

Several frowns later, she looked at him. 'But Robert,' she said. 'The money – we don't have that much, do we?'

'No,' he said cheerfully. 'But, well, first you have to see it. Then we'll talk about it.'

On Sunday morning they set off in high spirits, and the nearer they got to The Old Manor House, the more Grace realised this might be a turning point in their lives.

She was delighted with what she saw but the downturn was the effort to achieve their desire. There was much work attached to running this sort of hotel, which was not in the least like the Beau Nash, but would require great effort on both their parts. More personal effort, she thought ... the Beau Nash was such a commercial enterprise with all it entailed.

Much thinking needed to be done but there was no doubt that they wanted it.

'Could you tell us,' she ventured to Mr Ashby, 'what the price includes? Furniture, fittings – I notice you have some rather lovely paintings and antique pieces.'

This was Grace's field.

'The paintings are mostly copies,' Mr Ashby said. 'We had some of the originals but when my in-laws died, we had a bit of a rough time and sold some, but we replaced with copies. I'll itemise the furniture I am taking – one or two pieces, family pieces, but those are in my flat and the hall and lounge.'

And the money – the biggest problem of all, they acknowledged back in Bath.

'We would have to sell my parents' house in Brighton – that's been a nice little source of revenue – and get a bank loan.'

16

'So we are tied – once again,' Grace said.

But they knew in their heart of hearts that this place was their destiny.

It took ten months to sort out before they were in and settled. Their flat, unlike the one at the Beau Nash was on the ground floor and, when they finally took over, they stood looking at each other, unable to believe what they had done.

Robert raised his glass. 'Good health ... here's to the future,' he said.

'Cheers,' Grace said.

Chapter Three

Joseph Maxwell's office in the City was warm, luxuriously appointed and quiet.

Constance Boswell, seated at her large mahogany desk at the far end of the room, eyed the pink roses in the glass vase. She had left them there for Joe to see – a retirement present from the staff – he had missed the office party they gave for her the previous evening and was taking her out to dinner tonight.

For it had arrived at last. The end of the day, the end of her very last day in this office. Forty years – where had the time gone? She glanced at her watch – Joe would be here later today – he would be returning from his Friday game of golf, but he had spent the last four days in Finland.

She collected mail meant for his two sons, Gilbert, who ran the export department upstairs, and Graham, who ran the accounts. Her sturdy legs carried her upstairs briskly where Gilbert's four assistant ladies – his harem, the staff called it – also worked.

'Morning, Gilbert,' and gave him the papers.

'Ah, Miss Boswell, these for me?' and he turned his handsome face towards her. No one ever called her anything but Miss Boswell, not even Joe, in front of the staff.

'Dad not back yet?'

'No. All well up here?'

'Yes, thanks, nice party wasn't it?'

'Oh, wonderful. Thank you all so much,' and the girls – women all over fifty – smiled at her.

She looked at them from behind thick lenses. A nice bunch.

Gilbert was a handsome devil, she thought, nothing like his father to look at. He was married to a wealthy socialite and they lived in a London square. They had no children and, apart from the working hours which his father insisted he put in, they lived a life of luxury.

And down to Graham's office. Graham, a younger, leaner, more handsome version of his father, smiled warmly at her.

'So, it's finally arrived, Miss Boswell.'

'Yes,' she smiled, laying the papers on his desk.

'Anything important?'

'No, just the usual. I'll see you before you go,' and she closed the door behind her.

This morning she had thought, this is the last time I shall catch this bus for the City – the very last time.

Tonight Joe would drive her home to Clapham. And that would be that. She had been twenty when she first arrived at Maxwell's – a junior office girl. Maxwell's agents for paper and board mills in Scandinavia and Europe, import and export – and it had grown since she had been there.

She walked through the dispatch department. Of course, when she first joined the firm it had been called the post department, and there had been franking and weighing machines. They even had a commissionarie called Davies, in full uniform, a little chap with bright blue eyes, and a white moustache.

Well, it had all changed now. Margaret Church, who ran the dispatch department, was very efficient but Miss Boswell had never liked her. She made snide remarks about the rest of the staff and always gave more attention to the men than the women. She was pretty enough but with a thin little mouth, which was always shiny. Her sister, Kath, older than herself, worked in the accounts department, an extremely pretty girl. One day when she had rushed through the dispatch department to get to her office, Margaret looked up.

'Kath! You're late,' and turned to Miss Boswell. 'She came home at two this morning without her knickers, not that she usually wears any.'

'Objectionable girl, Miss Boswell thought.

Another time, Graham had walked through the office with a large envelope.

'Stiffen that up, Margaret,' he had said, and Margaret had licked her shiny lips and Constance had intercepted a look that passed between them.

Ugh, she did hope Graham wasn't up to anything, it would be more than his job was worth. . .

No, she certainly wouldn't miss Margaret Church. . .

She had watched Joe leave this morning, dressed for golf, a short, stocky little figure in his thick black Braemar woollen socks with green tabs at the side, the highly polished brogues, as he had left for what was to him the best day of his week.

Strange that all those years ago – thirty-five to be exact – they had had a passionate love affair. She had been with the firm for about five years when she became his personal secretary; he had asked for her particularly and she had been only too willing to comply.

She had worked hard at evening classes to perfect her shorthand and typing for this was the 1960s and the magical digital world that would open up before them had not yet happened. She had adored him, her first and only love. He had been strong and handsome, if a bit on the short side, with those twinkling brown eyes that could burn into hers over the desk, the way he looked at her. She was ripe for picking, a pretty little thing from Ilford, travelling up to town every day on the train. Serious minded, a churchgoer, she had been easy prey. It had started with a private dinner after working late, then some spark in both of them ignited and that was that.

Now she could only recall it with wonder. An illicit affair, she, Constance Boswell, with a married man. It was as if it had happened to someone else. His wife, Isabel, had borne him two sons, and Constance had though about them only briefly before tossing her bonnet over the windmill.

How wonderful it had been while it lasted – the intrigue, the secrecy, seeing him every day, the way his eyes held a passionate promise, the thrill when his hand brushed hers. Had they managed to keep it a secret? She would never know now.

She sighed, coming back to earth. It wasn't as if she often thought about those far-off days; that time in her life that was as dead as the dodo, dry as ashes in the mouth. When the affair had burned itself out, as it was bound to do, there was no question of her leaving. She was indispensable to him and she had settled down to what she had become – an elderly spinster with no time for anything but her job. Her life, she thought, given to one man. A man whose wife had borne him a daughter after the affair, a man whose only interests were his business, his children, his golf and the boat he kept down in Hampshire where he had a weekend cottage. But she was the undisputed boss of the staff. She had been brought up strictly. Her parents had both been in service before they married, her mother a lady's maid, her father a valet. When the war came, both left and went into the services; her mother joined the ATS and her father the Navy.

After the war, her mother had lost none of her ideas on strictness and protocol. As a lady's maid she had had good training and knew exactly what was correct. When every other girl was going mad in the 1960s and Mary Quant was queen, Constance wore beautifully cut tweed suits and real leather handbags and shoes. Not for her the mini skirts and bouffant hairdos – she was brought up as a lady should be – according to her mother's dictum. She smiled now. So much for that. . . When her parents died, she moved to a

21

flat in Clapham and every day caught the bus to the City.

Joe and his family lived in North London, the two boys were married, the daughter abroad, and Isabel had died two years ago. It was never mentioned between them. She recalled Isabel coming to see Joe in the office soon after she had been made his private secretary. She had always secretly thought that Isabel had come to look her over. Sussing her out, as they said today.

Well, she smiled to herself. She needn't have worried. I was not by any means the typical pretty secretary after her boss. Still, I had my moments.

Once, only a few years ago, she had been invited to his house for dinner in company with some members of the staff and some foreign visitors. The house was large, brick-built and comfortably furnished. She remembered her surprise when, on entering the dining room, she found the table perfectly laid with gleaming cutlery and snow-white napery but with coloured drinking glasses. A child of her mother, she was shocked. Red wine glasses, blue water glasses, pink glasses, exquisite on long stems but *coloured...*

She thought back to their small terraced house in Ilford, her mother's dining room laid for lunch on a Sunday, with shining crystal glasses and exquisite napery. She smiled now, thinking how shocked her mother would have been. Poor Isabel . . . and glanced at her watch. Joe was late. She got up and made herself coffee. Most of the staff had said their goodbyes and made their departures but she was used to Joe being late.

From her handbag, she took out the brochure from The Old Manor House. It was a luxury hotel in the Cotswolds and she had had her heart set on it for some time. She had booked in for two weeks, starting this Sunday.

Sometimes she had thought she would do a bit of travelling on her retirement. She had been to France and Italy but mostly she went to Cornwall. She was very fond of the British coastline and the country areas, particularly Dorset.

Had been, once, to Scotland. She had gone with a friend for a few years, Elsa, who had sadly died last year. Now she didn't much fancy travelling as a single woman.

But she had heard about this luxury hotel where they couldn't do enough for you and that's what she wanted. To be waited on, hand and foot, literally, and in such a lovely part of the world. It was expensive – very – but what was money for? She had written for the brochure and had sat up most nights studying it.

Now she opened it again. The Old Manor House. She had bought some super clothes and she would have her hair done tomorrow at an exclusive salon for the first time in her life, her nails manicured; she would spoil herself and she found herself looking forward to it more than somewhat.

Lost in a world of daydreams, she was startled when Joe came in, his face ruddy from the fresh air, small dark eyes twinkling.

'Constance,' he said hanging up his coat. 'All well?'

'Yes, fine, Joe,' she said.

'My word, what lovely flowers.'

'Yes, from the girls upstairs.'

He flopped down at his desk.

'Good game?'

'Great,' he said.

He gave her a quick glance then looked at the papers on his desk. 'Any messages?'

She shook her head.

'Still all right for tonight?'

'Of course, Joe,' she said.

'I thought we'd go for a drink before dinner—' then another quick glance at her.

'Anything you say,' she said.

He shuffled the papers neatly and put them in a drawer.

Another glance at her. 'You look very nice,' he said, appraising her. It was the first compliment he had paid her since their affair all those years ago.

'Thank you,' she said. 'I dressed especially knowing you were taking me out to dinner.'

'I booked the Ritz,' he said.

'Oh, Joe, how nice,' she said, and it was. She hadn't been to the Ritz since – well – all those years ago.

They sat drinking at the bar, Joe with his whisky sour, she had a gin and tonic. Sipping it, for she wasn't used to drink.

He told her about his sons and their children – his four grandchildren, of whom he was very proud. They talked as strangers, for she never saw him outside office hours.

Then they made their way to their table, escorted, for Joe was a popular diner – respected for his money and position – as well as his taste in food. He chose the meal, knowing what she would like, and they sat back enjoying the unaccustomed ambience while Constance toyed with her wine glass. All those years ago they had something to say to each other, now, he was like a stranger outside the office.

'Well, Constance,' he said. 'What are you going to do with yourself – eh?'

She smiled across at him. She did have nice teeth and a nice smile, he reminded himself, and she shrugged.

'I can't quite get used to the idea,' she said. 'I've worked all my life.'

'Not all your life,' he corrected her. 'Just part of it, the rest is just beginning.'

The waiter brought the first course and they were silent during the meal.

When the waiter took the dishes away, Constance dabbed at her lips and Joe wiped his mouth vigorously.

'I thought I would take a holiday,' she said and he raised his eyebrows.

'Holiday?' he said as if he didn't understand.

'Yes, you know, a luxury break – somewhere where I would be spoiled.' And she smiled.

'Doesn't sound like you,' he frowned.

They were interrupted by the arrival of the cheese board

after both declining a dessert course and busied themselves until the coffee arrived.

Then he looked over to her, met her eyes, those twinkling dark brown eyes – that bore into hers. His hand crept over the table and covered hers.

'I have a much better idea,' he said.

Her blue eyes were wide.

'Come and live with me. We shall get married. You know, Constance, I get very lonely at times and I am sure you do, After all, we get on together and there is nothing I would like better than to spend the rest of my days with you.'

Constance was astonished. This was the last thing she expected him to say. She left her hand where it was.

'Joe—'

'I thought, after this, we would drive back to my home – you have been there before, haven't you? We'll have a nightcap there, before I drive you back to Clapham. We'll talk about it, make plans.'

Into her mind flashed the sight of the dining room with all those coloured glasses ... red, blue, pink ...

She took her hand away – her mind made up.

The lights shone over in the park; never was there a more beautiful setting, she thought, a sense of unreality overtaking her. She had been here before during their five-year affair and wondered how they had dared. Supposing Joe's wife had come in ...

But Joe would be sure about that. Joe never put a foot wrong. Of course, he had been on his own now for two years, except for a housekeeper, an elderly woman who had been with the family for years. But he had his golf, and his family, while she ...

'Joe, thank you, I can't, I'm sorry, but I can't.'

His mouth was open, so sure had he been that she would accept 'What do you mean – you can't?' He was not used to opposition. 'Why not?'

She smiled across at him. 'Joe, I've booked a two-week

break, in the country, at a luxury hotel.'

He looked relieved. 'Oh, is that all!' he said, and smiled across at her indulgently. 'You can easily cancel that – no problem – or I'll come with you if you like. Where is it?'

How sure of himself he was, she thought, with a twinge of annoyance.

'Why are you doing this?' he asked.

'I don't know why, Joe,' she said gently, still smiling across at him. 'Just that I have to go, be by myself, do some thinking.'

'But you've lived on your own ever since you left school ...' He stared at her for what seemed like minutes and she felt a curious exultation inside her.

He beckoned the waiter over. Sternly he delt with the waiter's proffered book, then stood up.

She rose to her feet. Escorting her to the door where their car was waiting, he stood while she got in the passenger seat then got in beside her.

'Not much point in going to South Lodge,' he said. 'You've obviously made up your mind. I'll drive you back to Clapham.'

'Thank you, Joe,' she said, aware of a sense of excitement now that she had burned her boats.

He gave a deep sigh. 'Well,' he grumbled. 'Get this little break over and we'll talk again, eh?' as if he was talking to a spoiled child. 'You'll give me a ring when you get back?'

He went round and opened the door for her and watched as she made her way up the narrow path.

She turned. 'Thank you, for this evening, Joe. I'm sorry, goodnight.'

'We'll talk later,' he grunted.

She knew she had given him an awful shock – and disappointment too but she felt only elation at having stuck to her guns. As she went to draw the bedroom curtains, she saw him pull away from the kerb.

She sat down on the bed and got out the brochure. She

knew she wouldn't sleep much tonight . . . she was going to
The Old Manor House. She would get her little car out and
set forth on her very own adventure.

Thank heavens she hadn't been mad enough to book a
journey to Bulgaria or Peru or wherever. Australia, even,
or the Indian Ocean – no. She was far happier doing her
own thing here.

But imagine – Joe asking her to marry him! Something
she had never ever considered. Never thought she would be
asked. Now, though, it had come too late. A stepmother to
those middle-aged boys, the grandchildren – she shivered
slightly.

Watch your step, Constance, her mother would have
said.

Chapter Four

The Markhams had been at The Old Manor House for just over a year. Now, on this early June morning, Grace looked out on to the splendid gardens, ablaze with colour.

For the layout of the gardens was a speciality of The Old Manor House, an annual expense that they had never encountered before. Their previous hotels had seen nothing like this, The Swan had its window boxes and tubs and courtyard, being on the village High Street, while the land available at the Beau Nash was minimal. It had sported tubs and urns both inside and outside but this was different.

Leading up to and immediately around the house were beds full of colour, spring flowers followed by the summer flowering display. Three gardeners were kept in attendance, for people came from other Cotswold villages to see the display in Cypress Grove. There was nothing nicer than sitting on the terrace having coffee or after-dinner drinks surrounded by the scent of roses and honeysuckle. Robert and Grace never tired of looking at their garden. Beyond the flower beds stretched immaculate lawns, fringed with trees, now in their summer beauty, while the hills rose up behind them. The landscape disappeared into the distance, where cows and sheep grazed. It was altogether blissful and no one was more pleased than Robert and Grace to think they owned it – well, almost.

They had long ago decided it was best thing they had

ever done and their daughters, Molly, Alice and Jenny, all agreed. At quiet times, usually in the winter, they would spend a few days with their parents, taking a break from their own hard-working lives.

Walking into their bedroom from the bathroom Robert slowly got dressed.

'Miss Boswell settled in?'

'Yes – nice woman – and – his lordship arrives today.'

Robert smiled, tying his tie. This was a private joke because of the man's accent.

'Hasn't been before?'

'Not since we've been here.' She gave him a swift kiss and went on to begin the day.

Constance Boswell woke two hours later and her wide blue eyes sparkled. She got out of bed and pulled back the curtains.

She lay back, hands behind her head looking at the view through the window. She was on the first floor – there were only two floors used by residents, served by a small lift discreetly tucked away beside the wide curving staircase. The attic floor, as it was called, was used by the staff and a special lift out of the kitchen provided for that.

A small smile played around her mouth as she remembered her meeting with Joe. How pleased she was that she had stuck to her plan. Poor Joe – she could think like that about him now.

Her room was delightful. Furnished in blue and cream, it was just to her taste. Soft cream carpet and blue and white curtains draped and tied back in the old-fashioned way with heavy silk cords and tassels. All the rooms held two beds but were frequently taken by single people. At dinner the evening before she had seen four couples and two singles. An elderly man and an elderly woman at separate tables.

She was pleased that she had provided herself with some decent clothes. Her mother would have approved, she thought wryly, as she sat in her long black skirt and multi-coloured top. She wore her mother's pearls – the only jewellery her mother had left her, and wore no rings on her hands. Her bracelet was a thin gold band given to her by Joe on one of he birthdays during the height of their passion for each other.

And it had been a passion, she thought now, reflecting. If she had felt about him now as she had then, she would not have refused him. But times had altered – she had changed, as had Joe – this was another world.

She bathed and got dressed and faced herself in the mirror. She had no illusions. She was below average height but she stood well. Shoulders back – stand up straight – this from her mother, who was of the same build as herself.

Her large blue eyes were her best feature, although she wore glasses for reading but contemplated buying contact lenses in the future. She put on well-cut cream trousers and a thin silk top and navy jacket. Flat shoes – she had never worn high heels, although when she was younger she wore Louis heels. Her hair was still dark though there were traces of grey; she was pleased she had gone to the hair-dresser in Knightsbridge, even though it had cost an arm and a leg. Her teeth were good and she had a nice smile.

Could do with losing a bit of weight, though, she decided, patting her tum. Then, putting on a trace of lipstick, she went down to breakfast.

Not many about, but the waitresses hovered; she was offered various juices, coffee or tea or chocolate. She could have had breakfast in her room but chose not to. After all, meeting and mixing with other people was part of the holiday.

She helped herself to the magnificent spread laid out on a nearby table, passing the elderly gentleman she had seen the night before.

'Good morning,' they exchanged greetings and, over her coffee and toast – she was not by nature a breakfast person – decided what to do with her day.

She would take a walk around the village, explore, look in the few shops that were there. It would be as well to get her bearings early on – she could take the car and drive around during the next two weeks.

Leisurely, she walked out through the reception area to the back entrance that overlooked the terrace. All the tables and chairs were set for a sunny day, while the flower beds were riotous with colour. She took several deep breaths and walked round the flower beds and out on to the path that led down the little lane into the village. She crossed over a small bridge that spanned a narrow little stream; she wondered if it might be the River Windrush – she had read about that.

Even the air smelled good – so different from London. She crossed the road and on to the pavement that encircled the village green.

A newsagents, with lots of cards of the area, an antique shop – well, there would be plenty of those in the Cotswolds, a shop selling beautiful china, and then a very narrow lane, Lamb Street. On the corner was a tiny house called Lamb Cottage and she smiled. So sweet, it was like something in a fairy tale. There were lace curtains at the windows and, as she passed, she saw one being allowed to fall back. She smiled, and on to a rather gracious-looking house – pure Georgian. It was so elegant, with its front garden massed with flowers and pots of hydrangeas; everyone here seemed to make such an effort at presenting their beautiful buildings.

Some more shops, and then she was at the start of the cypress grove itself, which led up to the church. It was shady and cool, nice on a summer's day, she thought, and made for the church. The church was unlocked and she went inside. It seemed minute and she made up her mind to come to a service on Sunday. It was years since she had been to church although, until her affair with Joe, she had been a regular churchgoer.

Outside again she faced the little churchyard and

wandered round the tombstones, some of them dated hundreds of years since. Emerging through the gate at the other side, facing her was a small stone cottage and it had a FOR SALE board outside.

She caught her breath. Imagine – to live here – away from the noise and traffic of London ... Would she like that? She was free, free to do as she liked for the first time in her life. No office to get to, no ties, she was fortunate. No relatives, a few friends, but they would come and stay; she got quite carried away.

Granny Holden, still watching from the window of Lamb Cottage, saw her returning on the other side of the green. Nice woman, she liked the way she held herself. Walked proudly, back straight, she liked that. She'd ask Bernice who she was. Be bound to be staying at The Old Manor House.

She let the curtain drop and stood for a moment. In her eighties she still stood well, for she had been a dancer in her youth – gone away to London – although she had been brought up in this cottage, which had belonged to her grandmother. History repeating itself, she thought wryly. She had left Cypress Grove without a backward glance during the war, glad to escape to the life that was to be lived in London. Excitement, the stage – couldn't wait to get away...

She pulled the curtain straight and sat down in her favourite chair. 'Course, it was different then, the war was on, and the blackout but that didn't stop you when you were young. She knew her grandmother worried about her but, out of sight, out of mind. That was your motto when you were young. Those terrible nights during the Blitz, although they were exciting, yet terrifying – and then the Yanks had come ... Oh, what a time they had had ... Wartime London, when you skated so close to death some-times; it just added to the excitement.

Then meeting Buck, oh, but he was handsome. From

South Carolina. With that low, drawly voice, just like the pictures. They had fallen in love, really in love, not a wartime romance, and then, after a few weeks, he had gone to France and she never saw him again. Never knew what happened to him. She didn't think about those times very often these days, but she dragged a hankie out of her apron pocket and blew her nose. She was left, though, with a baby girl called Carol. And then it was home to her grandma.

Of course, she married – Tom Spooner, who worked at the woollen mill in Cirencester. He was a good father to Carol and when he died, well, that was that. Carol grew into a handsome girl, there was something special about her, and blow if she didn't do the same thing. Got herself into trouble, silly girl – well, she was a young woman by then – and goodness knows who the chap was.

Granny Holden got up and put the kettle on. It didn't bear thinking of really, because as soon as Bernice was five, Carol got a job to earn some money and disappeared, leaving the baby with her grandmother. She said she wanted to find her real father but, since she only knew his name and that he came from South Carolina, that wasn't much to go on. She heard from her from time to time but she never talked of Bernice. It seemed she had quite settled in America and never mentioned coming home.

She was always scared young Bernice would do the same thing – hike off to the States to find her mother – but she never spoke of her and never seemed interested in young men. But she was a good girl. Got a decent job over at The Old Manor House as a receptionist and she seemed settled there.

She herself was in her eighties and she wouldn't last for ever. Now everyone in the village was younger then her, most even called her Granny Holden out of affection and respect. Still – and she switched off the kettle and went to the back door to shoo the cat away.

Damned thing. Ever since that cat had come to live a few

doors away, she had lost her small birds. She had saved up for a squirrel-proof bird feeder because the squirrels were a nuisance and ate all the nuts, but the cat came and jumped on the wall, sitting there, alert and waiting and ready to pounce. All the bird food and nuts she put out couldn't bring them back, the blue tits and the robins.

She glanced up and saw the two collar doves on next door's cherry tree. Side by side they sat, one larger than the other. They had kissed each other over and over before he mounted her, then they sat side by side, close together, and it always brought a tear to her eye. She and Buck had been like that...

'Shoo! Shoo!' she shouted, and the cat swiftly disappeared.

I'll kill him one day, she thought, and now the collar doves had flown away. But they would be back...

Constance continued on her walk, still thinking about the little house. It would be wonderful – but she mustn't get carried away. She'd only been here a day. Besides, she was a Londoner by birth – how would she like living in a Cotswold village?

Now she had arrived at the village street and looked in the window of the dress shop, where several nice things were displayed. Well, that might be interesting. Next door was a coffee shop; she might go in there one day, on past the chemist and a shop with a wonderful display of rugs and bedspreads and embroidered pillows – she couldn't resist going in there. The bedspread she surmised was from China with all that embroidery but where would she put it? In the spare room? What a waste.

It was wonderful to have time to stop and stare and there were so many lovely things to see. The shops seemed different from the shops in London. Oh, and a charity shop, well, it would be hard to find anywhere without one of those. She walked slowly back to the hotel, where she thought she might have a sandwich lunch and a glass of wine. It was such a lovely day, she could sit on the terrace and, going to her room, she freshened up before making her way back downstairs to the garden.

She sat beneath an umbrella for she had no desire to catch the sun and there were quite a few people there. The elderly man she had seen last evening, who nodded, and two women who, she judged to be mother and daughter, they were so alike. Another tall thin woman, dressed in grey, with a patrician face, and the couple from the night before.

She had a prawn sandwich and a glass of white wine, then decided to have her coffee in the salon. The pretty girl was the one who served her at breakfast.

'Miss Boswell?' she said. 'Would you like coffee, here or outside?'

'Here, please,' Constance said. 'And what's your name?'

'I'm Mandy,' she said. 'I'll just get your coffee – anything special?' and, as Constance shook her head, tripped away. She's a pretty girl, Constance thought, with unusual colouring.

Looking around her, she saw now that there were several lovely paintings on the walls. They looked genuine but it was hardly likely they were. They would have cost a fortune. She didn't know enough about art to know herself. She would look on the walls going up the stairs – there was a wonderful collection. There were also several pieces of antique furniture around the room and it was so tastefully furnished.

She could see out to the reception area from the salon and saw a tall man arrive at the desk. He looked to be around forty, dark, extremely good looking; while the bellboy carried in his small suitcase doubtless others would follow with his luggage. He booked in – now he would set a few hearts leaping, Constance thought, and wished she had been younger.

But then, she thought honestly, I never would have attracted a handsome devil like that. I hadn't the appearance,

or the looks and I never did know how to flirt, and she immediately thought of Joe. He must have felt so awful when I
refused him, she reflected and had a moment's compuncion.
How would she feel at the end of the fortnight? Undoubtedly
she would see him – or perhaps he would sever all contact
with her. She had not given him the address of The Old
Manor House and he had been too sulky to ask for it. Forget
the City, she told herself, you are in the Cotswolds. Make the
most of it.

She saw the handsome man go up the wide staircase –
was he here on business? Would his wife join him? She was
of a romantic turn of mind and often conjured up other
people's lives.

She rested on her bed for half an hour, but she couldn't
sleep for suppressed excitement. This was a luxury she had
never been able to indulge in except on holiday.

She changed into a skirt and top and, taking her book,
walked down the stairs, stopping to look at the various
paintings on the wall. They really were remarkable, even
she could see that. Arriving downstairs she could see
several people on the terrace, some having late after-lunch
drinks. The mother and daughter sat at one table and
Constance thought what a very good looking woman the
mother was. The daughter had nothing like her good looks,
although it was apparent that she was the daughter. Not
quite the same lovely eyes, the abundant hair, the beautifully shaped mouth, the wonderful smile. It must be hard to
be like your mother, yet just miss the boat, she thought.
She had been like her mother to look at, in build and in
colouring, but she had her father's dark hair. Sometimes
she missed them, especially since she had grown older,
more than she could say. But her memories were wonderful.

The mother now got up and smiled sweetly at Constance,
who returned her smile. That was nice, while the daughter,
a little straightfaced, escorted her mother out of the terrace
and into the hotel.

She was joined at the next table by the elderly gentleman, whom she guessed to be about seventy but he might have been younger. He held out his hand.

'James Elliott,' he said.

'Constance Boswell,' she replied, taking his hand. How nice it was when people introduced themselves.

'Have you been here before?' he asked.

'No,' Constance said. 'Regretfully, I haven't, but I'm glad I came – it reaches all expectations.'

'Yes, it is a wonderful hotel. I come most years – my wife and I used to come regularly – and since she died six years ago, I still find time for a week at The Old Manor House.'

'I can see why,' Constance smiled. 'It is delightful. Just what the doctor ordered.'

He looked concerned. 'You have been ill?'

'Oh, no,' she laughed. 'Just one of my little sayings. I came down from London. It's lovely to be in the country.'

'Oh, how London has changed,' he said. 'I used to go up frequently but what with the traffic, and the noise and so on . . .'

He would be long retired, Constance thought. A widower. A well-educated widower. You were very class conscious if you came from London. The accent for one thing. He was a gentleman – or what used to be called a gentleman in the old-fashioned sense. Joe was a rich man, educated, a man who had built up a successful business, but she wouldn't have called him a gentleman. Like this man, who shrieked money and position. Well, it takes all sorts.

'Do you know the Cotswolds well?' he asked.

'No, not at all, I am ashamed to say. I have always promised myself a visit – but well, here I am.'

I wonder what he would say if I told him I'd worked in the City all my life and just retired.

Just then two women came out to the terrace, looking about them, both extremely well dressed and with happy expressions. One was quite large, a handsome woman,

37

her hair beautifully cut, her linen suit impeccable. They were obviusly friends, but the younger of the two was prettier. It was clear that the larger lady was in charge as she led the way to a shady spot and beckoned to the other one to sit down. Looking around, she smiled at all and sundry and waved to the elderly gentleman sitting with Constance.

'Mrs Collier and Mrs Baxter,' he said to Constance. 'They come every year, usually at this time.'

Lucky them, Constance thought. They were in their late sixties and were just the sort of people she had expected to find at the hotel.

He turned to her. 'Now, you must try and see something of the countryside,' he said kindly. 'Do you have a car?'

'Yes—' Constance said.

'Then you must visit some of the well-known villages – Burford, Stow-on-the-Wold, Moreton-in-the-Marsh.'

'The names are delightful,' Constance said.

'And so are the villages,' James Elliott said. 'Well worth a visit.'

He stood up. 'And now if you will excuse me, I shall make my way towards the new arrivals and say hello.'

She smiled up at him. 'So nice to have met you,' she said.

'See you later, perhaps,' he said.

It was one in the morning before Robert Markham came up to bed. He had spent two hours in the study checking the books and when he finally put out the light, the hotel was as quiet at the grave.

He made his way towards the flat and saw that Grace was sitting up in bed reading.

'You didn't wait up for me, I hope,' he smiled.

'No, I have a good book,' she said. He knew she would get up at six-thirty whatever time she went to bed.

'Everything all right?'

'Yes, fine,' she said.

'So his lordship arrived,' Robert said.

'Yes,' Grace said. 'Set a few hearts beating, I'll be bound.'

He dsappeared into the bathroom. 'Funny thing is, I seem to have seen him before, or his picture.'

'Perhaps he's an actor, TV?'

'May be,' said Robert, closing the door behind him. 'May be.'

Chapter Five

Anthony Sheridan followed the bellboy to the lift and found hinself in a room at the end of the corridor.

An old Etonian, Tony, as he was better known, was used to hotels like this – would have considered it beneath his dignity to stay anywhere else. After all, it was logical. If you were after big money, it was no good going to a boarding house in Broadstairs.

He flung his briefcase on to a chair and flopped into another, stretching his long legs. Well, let's see how this one worked out.

He got up after a minute and pushed the other window open. The view was a typical Cotswold view but he saw none of that. As long as the hotel was comfortable, that was all he asked.

Glancing in the mirror, he reflected that the journey had been easy. His car, his beloved Ferrari, and up to now his one indulgence, had stood him in good stead. He was handsome and he knew it. It was his stock in trade – that and his voice and his bearing. And now, he thought, for his next assignment.

Since leaving school – he had not been to university, deeming it a waste of time – he wanted to get out there and see what was going on in the world.

He soon found out. It took him no time at all to discover that if you kept your wits about you, were sharper than the next man, a better liar, then it was possible to get any woman if you'd a mind to; all in all, yes, he supposed he was lucky.

His parents had long ago written him off as the younger dissolute son; but he disagreed with that. He worked hard at what he did. If it didn't suit them, well, that was too bad and his education certainly had not been wasted.

Forty next birthday and it worried him not at all. His brain was sharp and active and provided his good looks and his charm held out, he had no worries. He had tried many things – a spell at acting, television, but, strangely enough, it had not been for him. Too much competition. A course at Sotheby's for which his parents paid, sure that that was the answer, a year at art school – he had learned a lot there, and it seemed he had a natural flair for art. Not as a painter but as a judge of other people's work, but he had no qualifications to enable him to get a job doing that, besides, the money would have been minimal. Given a choice he would have been an art restorer. But it was all too slow. He wanted a bit of life.

He had got in with one crowd who were intent on jewel robbery, which he found very interesting. But if you weren't at the top in that racket, it wasn't worth your while. You could say, he thought, that I'll try anything – once. And so far life has proved very fascinating.

A succession of girlfriends – they fell over in their exuberance to hook him – but not one that *he* ever really fell for. He had invitations by the score to stay in lovely houses and offers of holidays abroad; he was always in demand.

It was an older man who told him, 'In my day you would have been considered a roué', but he took it as a compliment. He was his own master. He had hordes of friends everywhere, from every class of society; he liked people and they liked him. In this he was fortunate in that he trusted people and never for one moment suspected that they would let him down.

41

Now he lay on the bed reflecting on the reason he was here. The previous week, he had been in a pub in Notting Hill with two acquaintances, Bill Mason and Alistair Summers, who worked for a prestigious interior decorator. They were experts at their job and were called upon to tackle many interesting properties. Not the sort of people you could employ on a shoestring.

At the moment they were engaged in redecorating a house of some substance, Charter Hall, near Oxford, which belonged to a Mrs Macready, a wealthy American widow from Wisconsin. It was her money that had enabled James Macready to rescue the old house from being pulled down and to restore it. Now, some six years after his death, she had decided that the whole place needed a revamp, as she put it, and was happy to leave it in the hands of Judy Sloane and her excellent team of artisans.

Mrs Macready, a woman of fifty-two, lived in the house with her only child, a daughter, Ellis, who was in her early thirties. Ellis was unmarried, but not for want of her mother's efforts, and the two of them spent all their time together: entertaining, travelling the world.

'You should see the place, Tony,' Bill said. 'Filled with antiques; she has no idea what to spend her money on next. Judy's on to a good thing I can tell you.'

'It will be easier next week with her out of the way,' Alistair said. 'She's going away and leaving the place to us – thank God. For a month, anyway, taking the daughter with her.'

'What's the daughter like?' Tony asked casually.

Bill looked at Alistair. 'You'd never believe in these days a woman could be so plain. The mother is beautiful, isn't she, Alistair? Mind you, she's fifty odd and she doesn't look it but the daughter – well, you'd go a long way to find anyone so – unappealing if that's the word.'

'But the jewellery must be worth thousands,' Bill said. 'Diamonds, rubies – I saw a lot of it while I was there – though she keeps it in a safe, of course. I heard she has some of the Russian crown jewels. Apparently her husband was a jeweller with businesses in New York and London.'

Tony never missed a word. He took a swig of his beer. He had no personal taste in drink – he just drank whatever his friends of the moment drank. It was easier that way.

'Where do people like that go?' he asked. 'Abroad, I suppose – Martinique, the West Indies, the Cayman Isles?'

'Well, no, not this time, she wanted to be on hand to oversee the work, so she's not far away. Funny name, in the Cotswolds somewhere, of course it would be a smashing hotel—'

'Cypress Grove,' Alistair said.

Tony gave a great sigh. 'Lucky them,' he said, downing his drink. 'Another?' he asked Bill, and Alistair nodded his head. Tony walked up to the bar, his head a maelstrom of thoughts.

Well, he'd a mind to take a chance. Truth was stranger than fiction, he had discovered. That slight conversation had led to this.

He glanced at his watch. Time for a shower, to be followed by the evening meal. There would be the usual people here, the same sort you found in every expensive hotel, from London to Timbuktu. That never worried him. He had a job to do. Still, if it was a waste of time, he told himself, you couldn't win them all, and he had only booked in for a few days. You never knew what was in store.

While he was in the shower he mulled over all that he had been told. He imagined the jewels would be worth quite a bit and it might not be easy to get hold of them. But he would enjoy this break and began to get ready for his pre-dinner drink, making plans at one and the same time.

Tomorrow he would make a round of the estate agents in the area and pick up particulars of anything prestigious they had for sale. That was what he was here for, if anyone questioned him. Looking for quite a grand residence. And why not? That way he would be free to come and go as he pleased.

When he was dressed for dinner, he walked down the stairs towards the bar, taking stock of the other residents.

Not many people here but out of the corner of his eye he saw two women getting out of the lift. Unless he was wrong, it would be Mrs Macready and her daughter. They fitted his friends' description accurately. The mother was certainly stunning, dressed in a long narrow skirt of emerald green silk with matching jacket, and wearing exquisite pearls around a slim throat and pearl earrings. She had a classical face, with high cheekbones, well-cut dark hair and her eyes were beautiful, long lashed, and they flashed a look towards him even in the bar – a look that told him she was aware of his presence.

The younger woman was obviously the daughter of this remarkable woman. Well dressed as she was, she was certainly without that touch of glamour that her mother possessed.

Presently two well-dressed elderly women came into the bar, obviously close friends; he knew the type well, and smiled back as he acknowledged them. Seated in a corner they ordered gin and tonics as he prepared to leave.

Once in the dining room he was led by a waiter to a single corner seat and asked if that suited him. From here he could see the whole dining room, and picking up his napkin, he prepared to study the menu.

Not many people, which was a drawback. Nevertheless, a single woman sat in the opposite corner from him, probably in her sixties, whose background he couldn't at the moment place. Judging by her expression she wasn't finding it easy to choose her wine. Nothing odd about that – it was typical of elderly lone women. The young couple, he would imagine were on honeymoon for it was a popular hotel for newlyweds.

He sighed and closed the wine list, hoping that things might look up before a few days were over.

Constance, it was true, never enjoyed ordering wine for

herself. Unused to it, sometimes she asked the waiter to recommend something and was usually content with what arrived.

She too, had noticed the good-looking newcomer; it was difficult to imagine what he was doing in a place like this. She recalled her walk of the morning and fell to wondering again if she might like to live in the Cotswolds. Really, it was an enchanting spot but then you would have to imagine what it would be like in winter. And, anyway, what did houses like that fetch in the Cotswolds?

Her thoughts were interrupted by the arrival of James Elliott who nodded to them before taking his seat by the window.

And then to the two women – obviously mother and daughter – what a regal walk the mother had. The daughter, who must be around thirty or so, looked sulky, as she had on the few occasions Constance had seen her, but the other woman smiled, not in the least put off by the sulky girl opposite her, inclining her head at the good-looking man and James Elliott.

Then the two friends came in, wearing long narrow skirts, and silk tops. The younger one had a good figure while the other was inclined to plumpness.

Constance, wishing to keep her weight down, ordered melon and salad. Cheese to follow and she would have her coffee outside.

It was so peaceful here, and so quiet. She wondered if after a time one might get bored but she was saved this evening by the two ladies, who smiled and asked, 'Do you mind if we join you?'

Constance gave one of her brilliant smiles. Ah, this was better. . .

'Please do,' she said graciously and they took their seats in the comfortable chairs.

'Now, I am Mrs Collier – Sybil Collier – and this is my friend Mrs Baxter – Katharine – well, Kath to everyone.'

'How do you do?' and Constance held out her hand.

'Constance Boswell,' she said as they instinctively looked down at her left hand.

'Well, Constance, it is so nice to meet you. Have you been here before?'

'No, I regret to say I haven't,' Constance said. 'But I am very impressed so far.'

'Yes, it's lovely, isn't it? A lovely spot, we always come at this time of the year. Oh, there's James—'

And he hurried over towards them. 'Ah, I see you have met,' he said pulling out a chair to join them.

'It is nice to see old friends,' Sybil said. 'Constance is new here, so—'

'Yes, we met yesterday,' he said, and Constance couldn't help but notice the little glances he threw towards Kath, who was the prettier of the two and the quieter.

'I see we have a new guest,' James said. 'I don't think I have seen him before.'

Sybil ignored this. 'Since we saw you last,' she said, 'we have been to Australia.'

'My word,' James said. 'A long flight, isn't it?'

'Yes, but worth it,' Sybil said. 'It was wonderful, wasn't it, Kath?'

Kath's eyes were dramy. 'Yes, but I have to say I liked New Zealand better.'

Sybil frowned. 'I liked Australia, so free and easy, if I'd been younger I could have stayed there, not that—' she began.

But James's eyes were on Kath. 'Could you?' he asked, 'have stayed there?'

She smiled at him. 'No. I like my homeland. I love England.'

'Oh, come on!' interrupted Sybil. 'You'd think butter wouldn't melt – but she's a real belter when she gets going,' and she laughed out loud.

They seemed mismatched, Constance thought, but perhaps that was it, the attraction of opposites.

A waiter arrived with more coffee, and all the women

accepted, but not James Elliott, who announced his intention of having an early night.

He pushed back his chair. 'Do excuse me, time for bed,' he said. 'Goodnight, ladies, I look forward to seeing you tomorrow.'

'Poor old thing,' Sybil said, clucking and looking after him.

'Sybil, not so much of the old, he's probably no older than we are.'

'Doesn't do to discuss age in company,' Sybil laughed primly. 'Especially women's ages.' She turned to Constance. 'Do you come from London?' she asked.

'Yes, I worked in the City,' Constance said.

'My goodness, that sounds very important,' Sybil said.

'I have recently retired,' Constance said, deciding that honesty was the best policy.

'And you decided to have a holiday at The Old Manor House,' Sybil said. 'Well, you couldn't have chosen anywhere nicer. We usually come once a year, don't we, Kath?'

But Kath was studying her nails.

The waiter arrived with more coffee.

'Are you going to do a bit of a sightseing now you are here, my dear?'

Constance smiled. 'I hope so.'

'There are some lovely villages – Stow, for one, nice shops there, and Burford. Do you have a car?'

'Yes, I drove myself down,' Constance said.

'They are very helpful at the reception desk – nice girls, aren't they, Kath? Bernice and Phyllida – been here for years. Brochures and maps and things.'

'Thank you,' Constance said, finishing her coffee. 'And now I think I am ready for bed . . . All this fresh air.' She smiled apologetically.

'Yes, make the most of it, my dear,' Sybil said.

As she left the coffee lounge the mother and daughter came in and Constance and the mother smiled at each other, but the girl scowled, her usual look.

Constance took the lift upstairs – and flopped on the bed. It seemed strange tonight – she felt herself miles away from London. And she had met the sort of people she wasn't used to.

Those two women – they probably had more money than she would see in a lifetime. Not that she was hard up, her pension would see to that and she had her flat which she owned. And she wondered again about the little house in the village.

She would go to Stow-on-the-Wold tomorrow and she had an idea that the board outside the house in the village named an estate agent in Stow. She must be mad even to think about such a thing. Still, after she had looked around, and had perhaps a light lunch, she would call in – it might be interesting. Tonight she was too tired to even think about it.

Getting up off the bed, she went into the bathroom. For some unknown reason she kept thinking of Joe. . .

Back in bed, she couldn't get him out of her mind. That last night – it had all been so quick, the evening meal, the drive back to her home, the proposal – for that's what it was. It had caught her unawares. In her wildest dreams she had never expected that . . .

She had been so excited about her projected trip, it had overcome everything else. All she had wanted was this holiday. Would she have felt differently if she had known it was coming? Joe's proposal?

She picked up her book but she couldn't read. Truth to tell, she missed the work at the office. It might have been a good idea to have spent a couple of weeks at home doing nothing before she came away. It was too much of a culture shock. She was used to dealing every day with queries, big business, had spent a lifetime at it. She would have to learn to relax. To be plunged into this sort of life was so different. This would be her life from now on: every day free to do with as she wished – she had not been able to imagine it. Then she began to worry if Mr Gilbert was coping; he had never been as good as his father around the office.

Oh, come on, Con, she told herself. Forget it. It's over. You are on the verge of a new life.

And, she thought, it had been her first proposal. Well . . . her first and only proposal. Only with difficulty did she at last fall asleep.

In their room, Robert and Grace prepared for bed also.

'How's it going?' Robert emerged from the bathroom.

'I think the Macreadys could be a bit of a problem: already she's lost something. I don't know what it was, but it's causing housekeepng a problem. I had to get Mrs Magnum to go up before she was satisfied. She insisted on the two chambermaids being called.'

He turned to her. 'What was it? Something important?'

'A pocket book, a diary, something. Anyway, not to worry, it was found exactly where she had put it, only she hadn't remembered where it was.'

'Yes, I had a feeling. Good thing they are not regular visitors. Their house is being done over, so they want to be nearby.'

'Yes,' Grace said, sliding between the sheets. 'Well, let's hope they soon finish it.'

Robert turned off the overhead light and got into bed. 'Incidentally, his lordship is looking for a house to buy in the area,' he said.

'Really?'

'So he told me,' Robert said.

'How interesting,' Grace murmured sleepily.

Chapter Six

Granny Holden was clearing away the breakfast things. She put the breadcrumbs out for the birds and topped up the bird feeder, not that it had been used all that much. The cat on the wall fled on seeing her, and she glanced up at the cherry tree. Ah, bless them, the collar doves, side by side . . .

It was later that morning when she saw the nice woman she had seen before stop her car on the double yellow. Oh, she thought, watch out, the traffic wardens are hot in the village, as she got out of her car. She was reading the sign at the house for sale and writing something down.

Surely not – was she interested in buying locally? Well, that was something to think about. But she was pleased to see the woman get back in her car before a warden came. She must get on. This afternoon was the meeting of the Women's Union and she always looked forward to that.

Constance made her way to Stow, out through the village, and down lanes – it was such a pretty run. Past cottages, where clothes lines billowed in the breeze, shirts and little jeans and t-shirts and gardens which were ablaze with colour. Up through another village and on – the sign-post said Stow-on-the-Wold, four miles.

She relaxed, no hurry. What was she doing looking around here for a house that was for sale? She must be mad. Still, it was intriguing. Not much traffic about – well, it was only ten-thirty.

She parked easily in the square reserved for parking and locking her car, began her walk. Lovely shops, selling all sorts of things. Rather like Cypress Grove, but larger, busier. A wonderful antiques shop and she passed a coffee shop advertising scones and cream – she might succumb to that later ... A large hardware shop and a chemist which seemed to stock everything you might want.

Under a lych-gate she walked up a path bordered by flowering plants, and then into a garden, obviously belonging to a hotel. Chairs were set out, and she sank into one and, when the waitress came out, ordered coffee.

Oh, what a lovely world this was. So peaceful. Tourists abounded, of course, and she wondered what it was like when most of them went home. In the winter. But she suspected that they still came, though in fewer numbers.

Only one or two people were having coffee, perhaps it was too early, and she fell to thinking again, as she had in the last two days, about Joe. Not only Joe, but the business. After all, you couldn't spend forty years of your life doing a job and forget all about it in a jiffy. Whether the bills of lading had arrived, the consignment from Finland – and she wondered what her successor would be like.

So much had been made of her own retirement that nothing had been said about Joe. After all, he was older, sixty-five to her sixty – it was time he retired. And he had his golf and his boat.

There had been no interview while she was there for a new PA. She supposed Graham would take his father's place when the time came. Thinking of the City she was suddenly glad to be where she was, in a beautiful spot in the Cotswolds, sitting in the sun, drinking coffee, and on her way to the estate agent.

Now, it seemed a ridiculous idea; but still she would go, nevertheless. Just out of curiosity.

She came out of the hotel garden and walked to the end of the street to another turning, just as busy. She could see the name of the estate agents hanging on an oval board.

Even the board was artistic, she thought, and went up three steps to the entrance.

The girl at the desk asked if she could help, and on being told motioned Constance to a chair to wait.

At another desk sat a man, confronted by – the good-looking man at the hotel . . . Well! She wanted to get up and run but asked herself what she was afraid of.

The hotel visitor stood up clutching an envelope in which he had put a number of brochures and held out his hand to the man across the desk.

'Well, thank you,' he said. 'I'll be in touch.'

On seeing Constance, for a moment he seemed surprised, then nodden and smiled. He held out his hand. 'You are staying at the hotel, I believe?'

'Yes.'

'Anthony Sheridan,' he said.

'Constance Boswell,' she smiled.

'Are you enjoying your stay?' he asked politely.

'Thank you, yes,' Constance said, and he smiled again. 'Good morning,' he said, and left.

Well, Constance thought. Perhaps that's what he is staying at the Manor for. Looking for a property in the area. Not unreasonable. Now the man at the desk was smiling and beckoning her to go over and take a seat.

'How can I help you?'

'Constance Boswell,' she said. 'Miss. I am staying at The Old Manor House and I noticed a small house for sale on the green in Cypress Grove.'

He looked slightly disappointed. 'Ah, yes, I am afraid there had been a lot of interest in that particular property. It is a very popular place to live, Cypress Grove and this sort of property does not come on the market very often.'

Constance waited.

'It is under offer – we have had two offers – but the owners are not prepared to accept them. So, if you like, I could always take you to see it.'

'And the asking price?' Constance said and when he told her almost swooned. 'Oh!'

'Prices have increased, I am afraid, to keep up with the general trend, the housing market has romped away.'

Constance knew it was well beyond her reach. 'Could I have the particulars?' she said. 'It may not be what I want at all.'

'Of course,' he said politely and from a cabinet drew a brochure and handed it to her.

'May I keep this?'

'Of course,' he said. 'And do get in touch if you wish to take it further.' He put the brochure into an envelope.

'Thank you so much,' Constance said. And armed with the particulars left the premises.

She went for quite a long walk around the shops, taking everything in. Well, it had been something to do. So, the good-looking man was searching for a property. Most intriguing.

She arrived home in time for lunch and had a drink and a sandwich outside on the terrace. There were quite a few people there, residents and non residents.

Early afternoon, and it was so peaceful. She thought of the crowded London streets; London was worse in hot weather – and sat back and closed her eyes . . .

Robert Markham came out of the little office just behind the reception desk and handed Bernice an e-mail.

'An American couple, a Mr and Mrs Dwight Warburg, are arriving on Sunday for four days. It was fortunate for them that the Martins have to rush back on Friday, otherwise I should have had to disappoint them. They're from Chicago.'

'Yes, Mr Markham,' Bernice said and she got to work.

'Americans, then,' Phyllida said when he had gone.

'Apparently,' Bernice said, busy allocating.

She looked up presently and Phyllida saw that she was lost in thought.

53

'I wonder you never wanted to go, you know—' she said.

'Yes. I know what you're getting at.' Bernice sounded bored. 'What's the point?' she asked.

'Well, it seems, when travel is so easy . . .'

The two had been friends ever since Phyllida had joined the staff five years before. Around the same age, they found they got on together, liked the same things, neither had a steady man friend, although Phyllida had been through a broken engagement. Sometimes Phyllida wished they could to on holiday together but that was not possible unless the boss got a replacement.

'It's not as simple as a flight across the Atlantic,' Bernice said, and she sounded annoyed.

'But, you know, to find your mother. It seems so strange – to have a mother – yet never see her.'

She knew it was a sore point with Bernice but mostly for her grandmother's sake.

'I'd have to go and search her out,' Phyllida mused. 'I couldn't bear it – not knowing what had happened to her.'

'Gran hears from her, sometimes,' Bernice said. 'And let's face it – I last saw her when I was five years old. I haven't a clue who or what she is and, as far as I am concerned, it can stay that way.'

'Does she never send photographs?'

'Who?'

'Your mother.'

'Not as far as I know,' Bernice was now looking a little cross.

'Sorry,' Phyllida said. 'I'm just being nosy.'

Bernice supposed it did seem a strange set-up to other people. For a woman to desert her small daughter and flee to another country to find her own father – she had never believed that as she got older. Her mother had just wanted to get away. To get as far away as she could from her own country and Gran, and her eyes softened. She thought the world of her gran – after all, had not she been a true mother to her?

54

She might take Gran away for a few days, if she was up to it. Eighty-three – but she was strong, kept going although she had had some disappointments in her life.

No, she would never leave her, as long as she was needed. She loved Gran's little house – had been brought up in it – loved the area, the life she led. There was always someone new to see at The Old Manor House – some very interesting people stayed there. She believed she was fortunate. Lucky to have a such job. There had been a short time of doubt when the Ashbys left as to who would take over, but the Markhams couldn't be nicer.

But then they were not new to the job – and Bernice knew that without contented staff a hotel wasn't worth a pinch of salt.

Sitting at the dressing table, Sybil Collier pursed her mouth in order to apply lipstick, while Kath sat patiently waiting. They would go down to dinner and have a drink in the bar, and both looked splendid in their long skirts and bejewelled tops, their rings and necklaces flashing.

Out of the corner of her eye, Sybil could see the set of Kath's chin and knew before the evening was over they would have an argument. And all because of that old boy, who unfortunately had chosen the same time as them to visit The Old Manor House. Come to think of it, she could have asked when she booked if he was going to be there . . .

Tomorrow they had planned to visit Berkeley Castle. They had been before, and it was a bit of a drive. Still, worth it when you got there.

And if he, the old boy, didn't suggest anything, she knew Kath would ask him to join them. Well, over her dead body . . . He would probably suggest to them that they accompany him on a run somewhere and she would be blowed if she would. Enough to ruin her holiday, him being there. They had met him before – last year, and it stood out a mile that he was keen on Kath. But she had not noticed it then. Kath was not averse to a bit of flirting, while she herself, well, she had never been 'like that'. She'd had a happy marriage but when Don died, that was that. But Kath, she had a way of looking at a man, oh, yes, Sybil wasn't silly, the way she crossed her legs and always wore expensive tights. And the little bit of cleavage she showed sometimes – but Sybil had had to tell her about that. Nothing worse, to see an elderly woman showing off her body – and she shuddered.

'Ready, Syb?' Kath asked, getting to her feet.

'Yes, dear,' Sybil said, smoothing down her skirt and linking her arm in Kath's.

Down in the bar, she saw him immediately. James Elliott, his stick by his side, at a table for four – you couldn't not join him – and yet – but Kath was going over towards him.

'James, how nice.'

He stood up.' 'Ah, I was hoping I would see you, do sit down. He waited until they were seated. 'Now, what can I get for you, ladies?'

'Gin and tonic for me,' Sybil said frostily.

'I think I'd like a martini,' Kath said, in what Sybil called her little-girl voice.

The waiter was at their side immediately, his head inclined towards James. James gave the order, and sat back, smiling at Kath.

Stupid old fool, thought Sybil.

'Did you go out today, James?' asked Kath.

'Yes, my dear, I did. I went for a stroll round the village – it was very pleasant. I hoped perhaps I would see you but I browsed among the books in the bookshop – he has an excellent selection, then I sauntered back, and had lunch – and I must admit to a little snooze and woke in time for tea.'

Kath smiled at him indulgently.

'When I got back from my walk I found a letter from my daughter. She is in Scotland and enjoying it very much.'

'Scotland is lovely,' Kath said wistfully. 'I have been there often, with my husband,' she added.

'We went two years ago,' Sybil said tartly. 'Can't stand the place myself – too many mosquitos,' and she sniffed.

'Perhaps you go at the wrong time of the year,' James said mildly as the drinks arrived. 'I am going to the Slaughters tomorrow. I usually go at least once while I am here. Would you care to come with me – such a delightful place?'

Kath visibly brightened. You could almost hear her reply, 'Oh, I'd love to' when Sybil's frosty voice broke in.

'We are going to Berkeley Castle tomorrow, some other time perhaps.'

Kath looked daggers at her. 'Well, we—'

'Oh, I mustn't disturb your plans, another day perhaps.'

They were interrupted by the arrival of Mrs Macready and her daughter, Mrs Macready in a wonderful outfit – a cream silk trouser suit which fitted her slim figure to perfection, while her daughter wore a long black dress.

'Well, I must say,' snorted Sybil. 'I have never got used to the idea of wearing trousers in the evening.'

'She does look smashing, though,' Kath said wistfully.

'Handsome is as handsome does,' Sybil said, which seemed to have no reference to anything, and then straightened her back and assumed a pleasant expression, as Tony Sheridan came in, nodding to them briefly before taking his seat.

Constance arrived wearing a black-beaded top and a long black and white print skirt. The outfit suited her and she was aware of it. She passed Tony's table, and he smiled at her and she thought, I am getting used to this, refusing to recall how much the outfit had cost her.

The young couple, whom everyone had assumed were on their honeymoon came in quietly, both of them serious faced. The general consensus was that perhaps the hotel was too elderly for them, it was hardly a swinging place – perhaps they should have gone to Majorca or Thailand – wherever it was young people went these days.

Martin was unhappy because Tessa was not happy.

They had lived together for three years prior to their marriage, as happy as a pair of turtle doves. They had been married the previous weekend, her parents providing a very expensive wedding indeed. They were delighted to see the young couple married at last. They had been waiting a long time for this, and now it had arrived. They had seen the young couple off on their honeymoon, it was a perfect ending; they hadn't said where they were going, keeping it a secret, but you could bet it was somewhere romantic.

The young couple had travelled all over the world one way and another and had decided that a quiet place at home, living quietly and in luxury was just what they needed – a respite from the long hours and pressure of holding down important jobs in the City.

Martin was delighted with their choice but Tessa, although she kept her thoughts to herself, knew that something was missing. There was nothing wrong with the hotel but their time together lacked excitement. She had looked forward so long to this and somehow it had fallen flat. Their lovemaking also lacked the excitement they were used to, and sometimes afterwards, she lay awake and longed for those stolen weekends, the atmosphere that surrounded their escape to their private world.

It had been no novelty – everyone lived together these days, but she had thought marriage would be different. She wasn't sure why it should be but she felt it should be. She twisted the slim band on her finger and, glancing at Martin, saw that he was watching her.

Impulsively, she put her hand out and squeezed his. She loved him, of course she did . . .

While Grace was in the bathroom, Robert checked the alarm clock. It was something they never needed but he did it every night.

When she came out, she picked up a magazine and made to get into bed.

'Did I tell you – a couple of Americans have booked in for Sunday?'

'No, you didn't. Well, that's nice. We don't get too many of those, do we?'

'That's true, he said. 'It's good news about Jenny, isn't it?' Grace smiled. ' Being pregnant? Yes, I'm really excited for them. They've waited long enough. I'll give her a ring tomorrow.'

Chapter Seven

No one was more surprised than Constance to receive an early telephone call from James Elliott.

'Good morning, Constance. I was wondering if you had any plans for today, and if not, whether you would like to come on a drive with me to the Slaughters?'

It took her quite by surprise and she had to think for a moment. 'Well, thank you, James. That would be very nice, I would like that.'

'Very well, my dear. I will meet you in reception at ten-thirty, if that is convenient for you?'

'Thank you, James.'

She felt quite flushed when she put down the telephone. Fancy, a date, at her age, and she smiled to herself. Well, she quite liked the old man, and she dressed carefully, putting on a cream skirt, a blouse and a cardigan, remembering that some elderly men did not like to see their companions in trousers. Her nice flat comfortable shoes, she imagined they would walk a little, but not too far, since James used a walking stick.

So it was with some excitement that, after breakfast, she sat in the lounge before making her way to the reception area, and found him already there.

He smiled at her warmly, getting to his feet.

'I don't think we are going to have any rain,' he said. 'Now wait there and I'll get the car.'

It was a nice car, a navy BMW, and soon she was sitting by his side as they set off.

'This is very kind of you, James. I don't know the area at all – and where – or what, are the Slaughters?'

'Delightful little villages, Upper Slaughter and Lower Slaughter. There is a very nice hotel there and I thought, if you were agreeable, perhaps we could have lunch outside. One needs to make as much of this delightful weather as we can. What do you think?'

She hadn't anticipated that but she had nothing else to do and looked forward to it. 'That would be lovely.'

They stopped several times on the journey, where he pointed out places of interest and in one village they had coffee in a pretty little teashop.

Constance felt so rested, so relaxed, it was a far, far cry from her usual life. She thought briefly of Joe and wondered what he was doing. Was he at the office, or playing golf? Who would have thought this time last week she was working in the City and she gave a brief thought to her roomy flat in the Victorian house on the tree-lined street in Clapham.

But then they were driving on again and arrived in Upper Slaughter soon after midday. The whole area was so pretty, with its little farmhouses and narrow lanes; there was a softness about the countryside. It was gentle, not dramatic like the Lake District or Cornwall, and then on to Lower Slaughter where they passed a beautiful country house or hotel at the end of a circular drive, and opposite another hotel, with a lovely garden, and a terrace laid out with tables and umbrellas.

Inside the hotel it was cool and comfortable and James suggested that they had a drink inside. The sofas and chairs were low and just asking to be sat in, somewhat like The Old Manor House she thought and looked about her, enchanted with what she saw.

He ordered drinks for them, then settled back, looking out on to the gardens, where there were several people, and

61

where the sun shone down on the flower beds. What a heavenly place, and to think it has taken me all this time to get to see it.

'Now tell me about yourself, Constance,' he said when the drinks came. 'I understood you to say that you had recently retired?'

She smiled. 'Yes, only last week. But I couldn't wait and booked The Old Manor House straight away,' wondering as she told him why she had done so and not given herself a week or so's grace.

Escapism, she thought, that's what it was.

'Yes, I worked for forty years as a private secretary in a City firm – importers and exporters of paper and board.'

'Forty years!' he said. 'You must have been very young when you started.'

No, James, she thought, I'm not falling for that one. 'Yes, I was,' and she smiled.

'And for the same firm?' he enquired.

'Yes, the same firm. Of course, I saw some changes during that time, as you may imagine.'

He sat thoughtfully. 'I too was in the City,' he said. 'In the bank—'

'The bank?' she said.

'Yes, the Bank of England, in Threadneedle Street.'

'Oh,' she said, impressed. In those days it would be more impressive than it was today. She passed it every day on her way to her office in St Mary Axe. How strange. She wondered what age he was. She felt he was a good deal older than she herself was.

'Did you live out of town?' he asked.

'Yes, I had, have a flat in Clapham,' she said. 'Not too far from the City,' and thought it was time she asked questions too.

'Did you have much of a journey to the City?' she asked.

'Well, originally, I used the tube, but in later years, of course, a car.'

And probably a chauffeur too, she thought.

'I lived in Kensington,' he added.

'Oh, not far, from the City, I mean.' Yes, she could imagine that.

'You are not married?' he said glancing at her hands, 'or a widow?'

'No,' she said shortly.

They both looked out at the view.

'My wife died six years ago,' he said.

'Oh, I'm sorry ... You must miss her.'

'She was an invalid for a long time.'

'Have you children?' she asked.

'Yes, two, and grandchildren,' he said. 'I have a son and a daughter. My son has two boys and my daughter one.'

'That's wonderful.' Constance said, and she meant it. She often regretted the fact that she had not married and had a family but, well, that wasn't to be the way of it. Things didn't turn out like that for everyone. Never even had a steady boyfriend – the affair with Joe had seemed to scotch that. She had never been that interested, although she like a man's company.

'We used to come to The Old Manor House, until the year before Dorothy died. She loved that hotel, and they always were very kind to her. And I still come every year,' he said.

To find a second wife, Constance thought, and wondered again how old he was.

'You don't still live in Kensington?' she asked.

'Oh no, we left there when I retired. I live now in Bramhall, just outside Oxford.'

'Oh, not far.'

'No, I like to come here when I can, often thought of selling up the old place and settling in a village here. But, well, perhaps I am too old to move now.'

Heavens, Constance thought, he could be eighty.

'Well,' she sighed. 'I think it is a glorious spot and I am so glad I came.'

As if he had said enough about himself, he smiled, and looked younger again, and she saw a twinkle in his eye, which was rather nice. At least he has a sense of humour.

'I think perhaps it is time we ordered – a sandwich perhaps, or a salad.'

'That we would be nice,' Constance said.

'And wine for you but I shall refrain, since I am driving,' James said.

They went outside for lunch and each had a prawn salad followed by cheese. The birds came and picked up the crumbs – what peace, Constance thought. I could live here – but she tended to run away with herself – it's like any other good hotel, waited on hand and foot, not quite the same thing as keeping a home going. Shopping, washing, housework – now, make the most of it.

If Joe could see me now. A good thing I didn't tell him where I was going. I have the feeling he would be down here like a shot. Then she told herself not to be so smug. Still, he had asked her to marry him.

On the way home James talked of other things. 'Nice little crowd in the hotel,' he said.

'Yes.'

'Some of them come every year – it changed hands you know, some time ago – and I thought it would never be the same. Used to be a wonderful manor house lived in by a family for generations but, well, things change, and—'

'Oh,' Constance was surprised.

'But then they turned it into an hotel and it was very successful until Mrs Ashby died, and it was sold. The Markhams have been at the Manor for about a year, and made a good job of the transition. If anything it is better than it was. Very efficient people,' he said.

'It must be hard work,' Constance reflected.

'Oh, no doubt about it. But like anything else, when you put your heart into it, it rewards you.'

Like I did, with Maxwells, Constance thought.

Noticing that Sybil Collier and Katharine Baxter did not appear that evening, James thought they must have had dinner outside somewhere after their trip to Berkeley Castle.

Tony Sheridan, dining alone, was contemplating the best move he could make to get to know the Macreadys. They had acknowledged each other when he came in, but that was as far as he got.

Mrs Macready looked resplendent in cerise silk with a cerise and black scarf around her shoulders and a heavy silver and black pendant around her neck.

The daughter, he saw from surreptitious glances, was as uninteresting as ever. She was as tall as her mother but there ended the likeness. Her hair scragged back; he wondered her mother did not make more of an effort to see her daughter was well turned out, but decided the girl was probably difficult and disinclined to be told. She wore no make up – or precious little – and a long skirt and pink sweater. It was obvious that she had a tendency to put on weight and, if he was being kind, he would say that she was a little on the plump side.

But the mother: fiftyish, he thought, but his thinking didn't lie in that direction. He was more interested in her jewels and how he might obtain them.

He decided that after-dinner coffee time was perhaps the solution and he would tell the waiter to present his compliments and ask the mother and daughter to join him. This decided, he tackled the cheese and biscuit selection.

He took his usual seat in the coffee lounge by the window and waited for them to come in. Five minutes after they were seated, he beckoned to the waiter.

'Would you present my compliments to the two ladies over by the pillar and ask them to join me for coffee?'

'Mrs and Miss Macready, sir,' the waiter said. He was not unused to these requests.

He did not watch the waiter, or the reaction, but saw

presently the two ladies get up and, escorted by the waiter, come over to his table.

'Mrs Macready and Miss Macready, sir.'

He stood up, waiting for them, smiled and inclined his head. 'Tony Sheridan,' he said.

Mrs Macready dimpled. 'Mary-Ann Macready,' she said. 'May I present my daughter, Ellis.'

He took her hand, which was limp, not like Mrs Macready's which was quite vigorous. You could learn a lot from a handshake, he thought. He indicated the chairs.

'Now, ladies, what would you like?' his incredible eyes looked into Mrs Macready's. My, what a handsome man, she thought. Even better close to than afar.

'May I order you a brandy with your coffee?'

'That would be nice,' Mary-Ann said.

He turned to the waiter.

'Not for Ellis,' Mary-Ann added.

The waiter disappeared and Tony looked across at Ellis. She had nice eyes – or they should have been, but they had no warmth in them, no depth. She could not have been more uninterested.

'Are you enjoying your stay here?' he asked.

'Yes, very much,' Mary-Ann said in her slight American accent. 'We live not far away – but have come here to escape the workmen who have descended on our house.'

'Oh?' He looked interested.

'Yes, Charter Hall ... Do you know it?'

'No, I don't know the area, at all, although I am hoping to.'

'Oh, you live—'

'In London,' he smiled. 'I have a flat in Cadogan Square.'

She smiled. Of course, where else?

'And your house is being redecorated, or are you having building work done?'

'Both really, an extension or rather a conservatory and after that the whole thing redecorated. I expect it will take

66

some time, it is always longer than they estimate.'

The waiter reappeared with coffee and brandy.

Tony watched him go.

'Quite a project,' Tony said.

The girl had said nothing. She had not relaxed even when they shook hands, as if she had not the slightest interest in him, and Tony was not used to that.

'And you, Miss Macready?'

'Ellis,' the girl suddenly said.

'What an unusual name.'

'It was my grandmother's name.'

So she can speak, he thought.

'What brings you to the area, Mr Sheridan?' Mary-Ann asked suddenly. She was never backward in the conversation stakes.

He sipped his brandy and when he put his glass down, answered her. 'I am looking for a house in the area – a country house.'

'Oh, very nice, in this area particularly?'

'Well, I have a large radius, it depends what they come up with. I have one to see tomorrow, in, he consulted his notebook – Dell Bank Common.'

She shook her head. 'Don't know it. Is it far from here?'

'About fifteen miles,' Tony answered.

'Oh, quite near,' Mary-Ann sipped her brandy.

'You are married?' she asked him, having no time for beating about the bush.

He shook his head, and knew what she was thinking. Is he—

'No, I was engaged but, well, these things happen.' He looked very sad, like a small boy and she felt she wanted to comfort him.

She was all sympathy. 'I'm sorry,' she said. 'The same thing happened to—'

But for once Ellis was quick. 'Please, Mom—'

'Sorry, honey, I—'

'I know, but – don't.'

A bit of history there, then, thought Tony.

'I shall be going over to Charter Hall tomorrow to see how they are getting on,' Mary-Ann said.

'Yes, I daresay you need to keep an eye on them,' Tony said, and made a quick decision.

'I have this house to see in Dell Bank Common,' he began. 'I wonder, Ellis, if you would like to come with me – for the drive? I have directions, but—'

She looked quite shocked. 'Oh well, I—'

Mary-Ann's eyes were glowing. 'That would be lovely, honey,' she said, 'and it would be good for Tony to have a woman's point of view.'

So it was decided.

You fool, Tony told himself, but he seldom put a foot wrong. After all, life at the hotel was boring and he had to do something with himself while he planned his next escapade. Getting to know the Macreadys was half the battle. A step in the right direction . . .

Oh, for a decent night club . . . how many evenings would there be like this?

It was almost ten o'clock when Sybil Collier and Katharine Baxter arrived back at the hotel. They had dined out in another hotel and as the doorman opened the door, Kath could see James sitting on his own in the vestibule with a brandy at his side.

She made a move forward.

'Kath!' Sybil hissed.

Kath turned.

'What are you doing?' Sybil asked, her brown eyes dark with fury.

'I can see James over there – he is on his own.'

Sybil grabbed Kath's arm. 'Let him stay on his own. You must be mad, throwing yourself at him.'

And propelling her towards the lift, she dragged her inside.

Chapter Eight

Dot Turnbull, mangeress of the charity shop, was late arriving that morning having been to the bank.

She was horrified to see the window already dressed by the two helpers and flung open the door shouting as she did so.

'Who's been dressing the window with artificial flowers?'

They looked at each other. 'I did,' Rosie Machell said. Both helpers were terrified of her.

'Fresh flowers, please!' she yelled at them. 'Take them out at once, and go over the road and buy fresh. I'll bring some from my garden at lunch time for the desk.'

'Yes, Mrs Turnbull,' Rosie said, already her coat half on.

'And what's this?' she was about to start another tirade, when the door was pushed open and in came a customer.

She smiled warmly. 'Good morning, Ada,' she said. An elderly lady, rather oversized, went straight to the skirts where the larger sizes hung.

She moved through to the office, and saw to the cash situation, making sure there was change and, whipping the two ladies into action, picked up the black bin bag by the door to the inner sanctum and looked inside. Poking around a bit, she said tersely, 'Bin it,' then picked up another, bringing out a navy jacket, encrusted with brass buttons and braiding. The shoulders were wide, and exaggerated as had been the fashion some years before.

'Well, we know whose that was!' she said and peered at the inside label.

'Looks like a twenty-two, but its only a twelve,' she said. 'Versace. 'She even pronounced it correctly. There were no flies on Dot Turnbull; she knew the rag trade inside out.

'That'll have to be fifteen because of the label,' she said.

'Who left this?' she asked accusingly, picking up a table lamp and putting it in the kitchen. 'No electrics, you know the rules.'

'And tidy those books, Liz,' she said to the other woman. 'They should be in alphabetical order.'

'OK, I'll just finish dusting,' Liz said. 'Do you want some fresh spray in the changing room?'

Dot Turnbull sniffed. 'I should think so!' she said in disgust.

The day had begun in the charity shop.

Soon after ten that morning, Tony waited for Ellis in the reception area. His appointment at the house was at eleven.

She came towards him, looking much as usual, except with a woolly cardigan thrown round her shoulders and wearing jeans, but they were expensive jeans as he well knew.

He gave her a heart-warming smile. 'Hello, Ellis,' he said. 'We have a nice day for our house-hunting trip.'

She gave a weak smile and followed him outside to where the Ferrari stood waiting.

You could see that she appreciated the car for what it was, but she was not going to say anything. He made sure she was comfortable and noticed that she was wearing an expensive perfume. Mother's idea, he thought.

They set off, taking the road towards Cirencester, and said nothing until five miles out of the village, when he asked her, 'Are you warm enough, too warm?'

'No, I'm fine,' she said. 'Nice car.'

Perhaps, he thought, she is inordinately shy. Strange

70

girl, for all that. He decided to say nothing except to make trivial remarks, commenting on the countryside, how beautiful it was.

'It's new to me,' he explained. 'I'm a townie.'

'I think we go right, at the next turning.'

'Oh, thanks,' he said, driving down a narrow lane which led to a common.

On the edge of the common stood a rather fine residence, Georgian, surrounded by a garden full of flowers and with impressive tall iron gates leading to a drive.

The gates were open and he drove through.

'I am meeting the agent here at eleven,' he said.

'I'll wait in the car,' she said.

He stopped the car by the front door and saw another immaculate car standing outside, a Mercedes.

'Please come in with me, I was hoping you would give me your opinion.'

She seemed pleased at that and followed him out of the car and up the steps.

He rang the bell and it was answered by a young woman, while a man, obviously the agent, stood beside her.

'Good morning, I am Tony Sheridan and this is Miss Macready.'

'Andrew Harvell, how do you do?' and the agent held out his hand.

The woman, having closed the door, said, 'I'll be in the kitchen if you need me,' and disappeared.

Tony looked around him, never having been so bored in his life.

'Well, this is the hall,' the agent began. 'Some nice features.' But Tony was looking at the pictures on the wall and the odd antiques lying around.

Ellis moved around as if she was actually concerned with what was going on. 'Where does this door lead?' she asked.

'To the library,' he said.

'May we go in?'

'Of course.'

71

'Bit small,' she commented, while Tony, who had not the slightest interest in the place, was looking at the collection of books.

After spending a few minutes in there they left to find themselves back in the hall.

'The dining room?' she asked.

'Though here,' the agent said.

It was quite a grand room, filled with ancient oak furniture, dark, with heavy curtains which hid most of the view.

'Do you entertain much?' she asked Tony.

'What? Oh,' he said, 'quite a bit, yes.'

'You might find it a bit dark, depressing, almost,' she said, going over to the window and pushing the curtain to one side.

'Nice fireplace,' she said as they left the room to go to the large drawing room.

'Oh, this is better,' she said, and Tony was again surprised to hear that she had a voice, let alone opinions.

The drawing room was quite grand but would need a complete makeover for most people and, since she had no idea what Tony's lifestyle was, she refrained from commenting. The agent was pointing out the age of the house and the magnificent ceiling, while Tony was assessing the value of the contents.

Walking behind her, he realised that there was more to this girl than met the eye.

'So up now to the galleried landing,' the agent said, as they moved up the wide staircase into the sumptuous landing, fully furnished with antique furniture. There was bedroom after bedroom, full of genuine antiques, but few bathrooms.

The kitchen was huge and archaic. Tony followed Ellis and the agent, hands behind his back and once or twice Ellis threw him a quick glance. Now and again he would ask a question but his lack of interest was obvious.

The agent decided that his client's American partner was the more interested of the two and decided to concentrate on her.

'The grounds of course are magnificent,' he said leading the way out of the front door to the paddocks.

Tony looked at his watch. 'Look, I'm sorry, I don't want to take up more of your time than is necessary, but it is not quite what I was looking for.'

Well, that was no surprise, the agent thought. 'Very well, sir. Please contact us if you wish to see any other properties,' he said. Tony held out his hand. 'Thank you so much,' he said, leading the way back to his car.

Once seated in the car, Ellis turned to him. 'What was all that about?' she asked.

'What do you mean?'

'You hadn't the slightest interest in that house from the moment they opened the door. Why didn't you say? Wasting everyone's time.'

Oh, a little firebrand, Tony thought, well at least there is some life in her. 'What about a spot of lunch – a pub lunch?'

'What?'

'Stop off at a pub, some wine, a sandwich?'

'Sure,' she said, and he felt the first glimmer of interest since he had arrived at the hotel.

Two miles across from the common they found the little pub. Chairs and tables outside, flowers everywhere and the old walls festooned with ivy and creeper.

'You sit here, and I'll order,' Tony said, about to disappear.

'I'd rather come inside,' Ellis said.

She followed him to a corner seat and picked up the menu.

'I'll have a beef and horseradish sandwich and a glass of red wine,' she said, putting the menu down and removing her woolly jacket.

Tony liked that – a woman who knew her own mind.

He brought the wine over and waited for the sandwiches to appear. 'What did you think of it?' he said, his eyes twinkling.

'What was the point of it – you had no intention of buying that house,' she said sipping her wine.

'Not that one particularly but I thought it sounded interesting when I read the details.'

'Would you want such a large house?' she asked him.

'I do as a matter of fact,' he said.

'Have you a large family?'

He laughed at that. 'No, but I need a country residence.'

The waiter brought the sandwiches and put them on the table together with the cutlery and napkins.

'I see, the English thing,' she said.

He quite enjoyed bandying words with her. 'And since we are being frank with each other,' he said, 'What makes you tick?'

'Is that a personal question?'

'If you like – and you don't have to answer. I wondered why you always appear so disagreeable.'

'Because I am, most of the time,' she said.

He was surprised at her frankness. Perhaps she just needed to be let off the leash from her mother.

She put both hands around her glass and for the first time a glint of humour showed in her eyes.

'How would you feel?' she said. 'With a mother like mine? Beautiful, confident, a wonderful dress sense – a mother who knows all the social graces – to be saddled with me?'

'So far,' he smiled. 'You are more interesting than your mother. Forgive me, I don't mean to be rude.'

'But you are,' she said, with American frankness.

'Have you never thought of living a separate life? Doing what you want to do – going where you want to go, being your age?'

'I'm thirty-two,' she said.

'So? I'm almost forty,' he said.

'I guessed that,' she said. 'But then, you've no complaints, have you? Born into English society, all the charm in the world, good looking.'

Oh, he thought, it was a long time since he had met such refreshing candour.

'I know,' he said, looking down, and for the first time since they had met, she laughed.

'But seriously, why do you go around with her all the time?'

'Seriously, she has the money. I adored my father and he would have hated me to leave her. She is not quite as sure of herself as she looks and sometimes I think she enjoys having me as a hanger on, as it were. I am a companion to her, no trouble.'

'But you have a life as well and, if you will forgive me, you don't bother much about yourself. Does that sound unkind?'

'Yes, it does, but you're right. She long ago gave up the idea of trying to dress me like her little daughter. Besides—'

'Besides what?' He was really interested now. He had never met any girl so frank and outspoken.

'I've had my fling, if that's what it was. When I was nineteen.'

She was probably glad to speak her mind to someone, he thought, and for a brief time found that for once he was not thinking about himself.

She stared out to the Cotswold countryside. 'I was at university,' she said. 'I met this boy – he was from New York – outside our social scene. Do you understand?'

'Oh yes, it goes on here, too,' and he smiled.

'He was really really poor, no future to speak of, at least that's what my family thought. We were together for two years, until we left college and I took him home.'

'My parents – you've gathered I was an only child – were quite simply horrified. Even my darling father. This was something he would not allow. Well, to cut it short, I left and lived with Johnnie for a year in New York, until he left me, for someone else, from his own background. And it was a shock. I went home and I stayed there.'

She looked into the distance. 'Perhaps that was the turning point – I should never have done that but I did and here I am. My one and only excursion into the romantic world of love,' her mouth twisted.

'I can't forgive them though. It's true, Johnnie wouldn't have fitted into our world but we could have gone anywhere – and well, that was that. Since then I've gotten more – hard? – tough, shall we say.'

He was studying her, her face, her expression, the way she sat slumped – it was so alien to the way he was made – yet he had a feeling of pity for her.

'Yet, you have everything, ostensibly,' he said.

'And nothing,' she replied.

'Your Johnnie is not the only man in the world.'

'He was for me,' she said.

'Perhaps you don't have the necessary—'

'Courage? To face life? Perhaps, it's easier this way. This way I tag on, take the line of least resistance, you might say.'

'What a waste of a life!' he said.

'Is yours any better?' she asked. 'At the end of the day?'

He thought. 'Yes, I think it is. I am free to do as I like.'

'You think so – but you are always at someone's beck and call.'

'I am my own master—'

'I wonder,' she said and took a deep breath. 'I have a lovely home, money, an adoring mother, no wretched husband or lover to tell me what to do.'

'Only your mother to tell you what to do,' he said and suddenly got tired of the emptiness of it all. What was he doing here talking to this scatter-brained young woman who hadn't the sense she was born with – or had she?

'Anything more?' he asked. 'Another glass of wine?'

'No thanks,' she said and, getting up, picked up her cardigan and made to leave.

'Thanks for the lunch,' she said, over her shoulder.

Driving home, they were silent. There seemed to be

nothing more to say. He had forgotten by the time they reached the hotel what they had gone for in the first place.

Later, he flung himself down on the bed and closed his eyes. What a mess up – what was he doing here – he had made plans, schemed.

That extraordinary young woman kept appearing before him as he went through the visit he had made to the country house. He had never met anyone like her before. There was simply nothing about her that would endear her to a man. And, what's more, he had balled the whole thing up. But just what did he have in mind regarding the jewels?

In the first place if they were at Charter Hall, there would be no way he could get at them with his friends the decorators being in situ. Secondly, if she had them with her they would be kept in the hotel safe. How difficult would that be? If he became friendly enough with the pair of them to be invited to their room, what was the chance of getting hold of anything?

All in all it was one of the occasions that he had not thought through. He was having a bit of a break though, not to forget that. But back to jewellery: he'd sworn he wouldn't get involved again. The only time he had been was when he almost became a member of one the most expert gangs in the country. They hadn't quite trusted his lack of experience but gave him the job of lookout. He had had to hang about Knightsbridge. They thought he would go unnoticed there, keep an eye out, as it were, until such time as he gave them the all clear. That was all. They had made off with a fortune and he had seen nothing of that.

It was his testing time, they told him. For weeks he had wondered if the police might get in touch but they never had. He had decided then to be in charge of his own scams; he wasn't built to be a member of a gang. He was better playing it alone.

Now, he decided to go for a swim. So far he hadn't tried the hotel swimming pool, which was downstairs, and he knew it was small, but he doubted there would be many there at this time of day.

In his dressing gown he made his way down the wide staircase, passed the long high walls which were encrusted with paintings of every description. A few originals, but many reproductions. He had heard the story of the previous owner's collection.

He glanced at them as he went down the stairs, very fine. He would take stock of the others on his way back to the first floor.

Constance Boswell had had an afternoon nap, a sleep in which she had seen stained-glass windows and coloured glass of every description.

She woke, not knowing where she was, and sat up, her heart pounding, before realising that she was in the hotel and had been dreaming.

Whew! she wondered. Now what brought that on? She lay for a while trying to collect her thoughts.

It wouldn't do any harm to lie and think about things. She had been in such a hurry to get away, whereas if she had given it any thought she would have had a week or two at home.

She as not sorry she had come to this pretty village – it was another world to her. And she smiled as she recalled her trip out with James – and the two ladies – one of whom anyway had a soft spot for him.

She remembered the feeling. She had been madly in love with Joe. No good reflecting now that it had been a transient affair, a fly-by-night thing – they had been seeing each other for five years. Away from the office and outside. How had they managed that? What did his wife think? What excuse had he made – working late, pressure of business?

She herself had never given much thought to poor Isabel. As far as Constance was concerned she was way out of the picture with her sons and her lifestyle. And yet she had been there, in the background. I was a selfish little so and so, she thought now. But Joe was a strong man and I was willing to be led . . .

I wonder, she thought now, what would have happened if I had said yes to his proposal of marriage. I can't believe now he ever asked me – but he did.

And come to think of it – what am I going to do with myself when I get home? This blissful state can't go on for ever. And as for moving to the country – no, I am a city bird. A sparrow. It's too late for change now.

But I will have to do something with my life. Social work, a temporary job? I'd be lost without all that business acumen I possess. But it's time for a break. After the weekend I will be into my second week and thinking about going home. But there's lots of time yet. She got out of bed and went over to the window, where the sun shone down on the flower beds and, away in the distance, the sheep and cows could be seen. Her bedroom overlooked the terrace and there were a few people having tea.

That might be a good idea. She decided to change and freshen up and make her way downstairs to the terrace.

Standing on the stairs was Tony Sheridan – gazing hard at the pictures on the walls. He seemed startled to see her behind him.

'I'm sorry,' he said, allowing her to pass. 'I was just looking at these – er—'

'Yes, some of them are beautiful. I don't know a lot about paintings but you can see these are good.'

'They are mostly reproduction.'

'Really?' Constance said, looking hard. 'Amazing,' and walked on down the stairs.

Tony, left on the staircase, was engrossed in a tiny picture high up on the wall. If he could have reached it he would have taken it off its hanger and examined it more closely. But it was too far up.

He could have sworn it was an original self portrait of Dudemeyer. But someone was behind him and he made a mental note to come again and inspect it more closely. It wasn't easy with people coming and going all the time.

Once outside he quickly assessed the people there. The two middle-aged ladies, and James, of course. He seemed always to be there but no sign of the Macreadys. Just as well.

He decided to take a turn around the village, and passed the little shops. At the dress shop an attractive lady was dressing the window and she had some very nice things. He was surprised. Ellis could do with a visit there. These villages were not as dull as you might imagine. Which reminded him he must make an appointment to see Lucknow Grange, must keep his hand in regarding the purchase of a house ... that's what he was supposed to be here for, after all.

This time, though, he would not ask Ellis Macready. He would ask the receptionist which way to get there having received a telephone call about the property and the details. Perhaps that would be more suitable, he thought, quite forgetting that he wasn't looking for a house anyway.

He would go on Friday and, on the spur of the moment, decided to go back to town tomorrow. Yes, the whole thing was beginning to pall. A day in London was just what he needed.

The dress-shop lady as she was known generally throughout the village finished dressing the window and went outside to inspect it.

Pleased, as she usually was, she went back into the shop.

Tonight, Alan would call in, and she was always pleased to see him. Sometimes she got quite lonely on her own; but better that than ...

Genella had been a model in the early 1980s, that is, until she had met Alan Bembridge. It wasn't usual to live together in those days and they became engaged. She had no family but Alan had a large family and took her home to meet them. She liked them all, and they made her so welcome, thrilled to have a model in the family, and Alan couldn't believe his good fortune.

They were married the following June, she a vision in her bridal gown, and Alan so handsome. Altogether it was a fairy-tale wedding and a year later little Elizabeth was born. But she was born with a damaged heart and lived only five months.

Genella was completely devastated, quite unable to accept the situation. The problem was compounded by the fact that she could have no more children. This played on her mind to such an extent that she brooded more and more, until, after three years and a nervous breakdown even Alan had to admit that they had no future together.

All marital relations had ceased after the baby was born and although Alan persuaded her to see a psychiatrist, after which she accepted the situation, still he could not. Another year passed and regretfully he accepted that the marriage was over.

Genella knew, coming from a large family he passionately wanted children, and was anxious not to deprive him of them. So somewhat reluctantly, she agreed to a divorce.

Genella had come from the Cotswolds and decided that she would leave London and buy a small dress shop which was for sale in Cypress Grove. She had a small terrier, called Charlie, who followed her every where and sometimes, like this evening, Alan would call in, and they would pass a pleasant hour together.

She got out the glasses now and put them on the tray together with olives and nuts and bits and bobs. He never stayed for a meal. She was always happy to see him, although their recent life together seemed like something in a dream. She would have been surprised to know that Alan felt differently.

Yes, he had wanted children, and by now had two, but closest to his heart was Genella. What irony of fate had taken charge of their lives, he wondered. It had been almost too promising from the beginning. He rang the bell, and she pressed the intercom.

They kissed lightly and he saw that her hair was done differently. He still thought she was the most beautiful woman he had ever seen.

'Come on in,' she said. 'Nice to see you. Down, Charlie.'

Alan smiled and lifted the little dog on to his knee. It didn't do to think too much about what might have been.

'Well, how is it going?' she asked, knowing that he had been busy with a merger of two companies.

'Fine, so far, no problems,' he said. 'And how have you been?'

'Busy,' she said. 'Quite a few people in.'

'That's great,' he said. 'I thought the window looked good.'

'Thanks, I did it today. How's Myra?'

'Well,' he said, looking down and patting the little dog. This wasn't the time to tell her, if ever, that Myra was pregnant again, even if she was forty-two.

'Why don't you take a holiday?' he asked 'A cruise?'

'I might,' she said. 'But I hate to leave the shop. I'd really rather go in the winter when it's quiet.'

'Yes, there's some point in that,' he said.

She wasn't badly off financially, he had seen to that, with Myra's agreement, and she had the shop, but he felt responsible for her.

They chatted for a while then, as he finished his drink he stood up. 'Well, I'd better get back. Look after yourself,' he said.

'You too,' she said, and waited at the top of the stairs to see him leave.

What sort of fate decreed we should live like this, he thought on his way back to the car park. He would have given anything to have her back ...

Back in their flat, Grace sat at the dressing table soothing cream over her hands.

I had a call from Jenny, today, Robert,' she said. 'She's had her scan and she says it's a girl. She can't tell Paul,

82

since he doesn't want to know. Aren't they funny?'

'Well, we didn't have a choice in our day,' Robert said. 'I don't know that I'd want to know now.'

'I wouldn't,' Grace said. 'That's part of the surprise.'

'By the way,' Robert said, untying his tie. 'His lordship is viewing Lucknow Grange on Friday.'

'Oh, is it up for sale, then?'

'Must be.'

'That must mean the Levesons are going then. We shall lose some valued diners.'

'The new people may be even better.'

He leaned over to kiss her. 'True,' she said, getting into bed.

Chapter Nine

Driving towards Charter Hall with Ellis beside her, Mary-Ann Macready decided the time had come to ask her daughter about her day with Tony Sheridan.

She had deliberately not done so earlier, knowing how difficult Ellis could be if she was questioned, particularly on things she did without her.

'How did your day go with Tony Sheridan?' she asked casually as they came to a cross road.

'Oh,' as if she was miles away. 'Fine, it wasn't far.'

'How was he? Did he like the house?'

'He was fine and no, he didn't go for the house.'

Mary-Ann moved on. It was like pulling teeth trying to get an answer from Ellis. 'What was wrong with it?'

'There was nothing wrong with it, Mother, it just wasn't the sort of house he was looking for.'

'Was it large?'

'Yes, Georgian, but not his sort of thing, apparently.'

Mary-Ann drove on quite a bit further before she ventured again. 'What sort of man is he?'

'How would I know?' Ellis said ungraciously.

Mary-Ann sighed. 'You know what I mean. You know you could so something there if you bothered yourself.'

'Like what?'

'Well, play your cards right, he's quite a catch.'

'Here we go again!' Ellis said.

'I don't understand you, Ellie. You're not a bad-looking girl, given the right clothes and attitude – you could still make a good marriage.'

'Mom, could we stop this please?' What was the use of trying to talk to her?

Mary-Ann drove on for another five miles, before speaking again. 'I told you I was staying overnight, didn't I?'

'Yes, you did.'

'So you can drive the car back to the Manor and Jack will drive me back tomorrow evening. I'm going to a rather important dinner at the college.'

'Yes, I know, Mother.'

'You could have come.'

'I didn't want to.'

On the approach to Oxford, she took a left-hand fork and drove for some three miles before coming across Charter Hall, which stood in the midst of its glorious grounds. As they approached the wide gates, there was evidence of builders and workmen everywhere: scaffolding and builders' materials, piles of sand and cement bags.

'I wish now I'd stayed at the Manor. I hope my bedroom is free but I wanted to see how they're getting on. My goodness, it looks different already. Besides, there were some things I wanted to check.'

As she drove round the back of the house to park, she thought, as she always did – what a pleasure this house always gave her and having the wherewithal to improve it made it even more desirable.

Two large dogs came bounding out of the house and at the sight of them Ellis's normal expression changed to one of sheer delight. Sometimes, Mary-Ann thought they were all she cared about.

'Oh, you darlings!' Ellis said hugging them, as they jumped around her, obviously delighted to see her as she collected things from the car.

They followed her into the house, madly excited.

'I won't stay long,' she said. 'I just want to get some

books from the study and one or two clean things.'

'Have some coffee while you're here and see what they've done,' Mary-Ann said. 'Bring my case. You did get the jewellery box from the hotel safe?' She looked worried for a moment.

'Of course, Mother,' Ellis said. 'It's here.'

'Mrs Banks will make us coffee. Ah, here's Alistair.'

She was lucky that Mrs Banks, the housekeeper, stayed in residence while the work was going on, and that her husband, Tom, the gardener, would be there at night, while the two dogs were marvellous guard dogs.

Alistair greeted her and was joined by Bill.

He was smiling, so she assured herself, things must be going well.

Ellis walked through the house looking around her and going out through the back entrance. The dogs walked with her. She loved this house – everything about it – yet somehow she was enjoying her stay at The Old Manor House.

That evening the absence of two people – Mary-Ann Macready and Tony Sheridan – was noticeable.

After dinner, Constance decided to have coffee in the lounge and, seeing the girl, Ellis, without her mother, asked her to join her.

Somewhat grudgingly, Ellis did. She preferred her own company, which Constance sensed, but that attitude often hid a lot of disturbed thinking, as she knew from experience.

'Did you do somewhere nice today?' she asked pleasantly. Constance was a warm person with a generous personality and a comforting manner, especially to someone younger.

'We went home, Mother and I, to see how the workmen are getting on at Charter Hall.'

'Quite an upheaval, I expect,' and Constance smiled.

'Yes, it is going to be wonderful, I think. My mother is

always full of ideas, which luckily she can afford to carry out, so we shall see.'

'Your mother is a widow, I take it?'

'Yes, my father died six years ago. I still miss him,' she said.

And obviously was more fond of him than her mother, Constance thought, which was often the way with daughters. 'Are you enjoying your stay at the hotel?'

'Yes, it's quite nice, although I would prefer to be home,' Ellis said. It was hard going making conversation with her.

'Do you have a job, or work at anything?' Constance asked, quite politely.

Ellis turned to face her. 'I am always being asked that question but I have plenty to do at the house. Mother always needs help and it is quite a large estate.'

'How wonderful,' Constance said, for she thought it was. Freedom, living in a lovely house – as a working Londoner, she could think of nothing nicer.

They were interrupted by the sound of voices, which turned out to signal the arrival of the two middle-aged women friends.

Sybil Collier and Katharine Baxter were already arguing as they entered the coffee lounge and their conversation was audible from where Constance and Ellis sat.

They nodded to each other, then passed on.

'And I just hope, Kath, that you'll see sense about this. It is quite ludicrous – driving you over for a visit to his home – what on earth for?'

'He doesn't live that far away,' Kath said.

'So what? What's the point? Leaving me on my own all day while you gallivant—'

'You could have come too.'

'I wasn't asked!' Sybil sniffed. 'Besides, what on earth would I want to go there for? I am on holiday, for goodness sake.'

'So am I and I thought it might be nice—'

'Nice!' Sybil exploded, as they found a seat and sat down. 'I'm disappointed in you, Kath! I really am! You would never think we were lifelong friends—'

'Not lifelong—' Kath murmured.

'Well, almost, but you can count me out,' Sybil said. 'I've something better to do than gallivant around with an old boy like that—'

'I wish you wouldn't keep referring to him as an old boy – he's about our age. Well, a little more—'

'Is that what he told you? Some hopes!' Sybil jeered.

She took out a hankie and dabbed at her nose. She sniffed. 'If that's what you want to do, go ahead and do it but count me out.'

Kath looked down at her nails just at the moment that James Elliot entered the lounge from the dining room. Nodding to Constance and Ellis, he walked over to join the two women.

'Ah, there we are, have you ordered?'

'Not yours,' Sybil said.

He ignored the jibe. 'Coffee, black, please,' he said to the waiter. 'Now, ladies, where were we?'

It was a lovely summer evening as Genella Hastings left the dress shop with Charlie to take him for a run on the green.

Nothing nicer than a turn on Cypress Grove, where there were one or two seats on the triangular lawn, a few blossom trees, and the chance to sit and watch the world go by. It was usually quiet in the evening, and this evening, having arrived on the green, Genella walked the little dog round the green sward before settling on the seat by the cottage, which was still for sale.

She wondered about this, as did all the villagers – no SOLD board yet – and saw that a man was sitting on the seat opposite her reading a newspaper. A few yards away, a small boy played. She guessed he would be about five or six, and she smiled to herself. Charlie lay at her feet snoozing, occasionally lifting his head to look around, before dropping off again.

The little boy had a ball, which he threw and caught, sometimes going over to the man, who appeared to be his father.

Presently the boy came over to her. 'Hello,' he said. 'What's his name?'

'Charlie,' Genella said. 'What's yours?'

'Mark.'

'And how old are you?'

'Six,' he said. 'Well, nearly. That's my daddy over there.'

She smiled. He was a nice little boy, friendly. 'Do you live in Cypress Grove?' she asked him, and he thought hard for a long time.

'No,' he said at length. 'Do you?'

'Yes,' she said.

'Have you got a little boy?' he asked, sitting at her feet.

'No, I'm sorry to say, I haven't,' Genella answered.

'I could come and live with you and do your washing up,' he said.

'Really?' she said, slightly nonplussed. There was nothing shy or nervous about him.

'I'm very good at helping,' he said.

'I'm sure you are,' she said, looking across and seeing that the man was folding his paper and making towards them.

Close to, he wasn't that young, tall and good looking, his hair brushed back off his forehead, very blue eyes with a glint of humour in them, and a nice smile.

'Sorry, I hope he isn't being a nuisance,' he said, and held out his hand. 'George Turnbull,' he said.

She took his hand. 'Genella Hastings.'

'That sounds familiar,' he said.

'I own the dress shop – Genella,' she said, 'in the High Street.'

'Oh yes, that's it, that's where I've seen it. May I?' he asked, about to sit down.

'Of course.'

The boy bent down to talk to the dog.

'Is he safe – your little dog?' George asked.

'As a rule; he doesn't meet many small boys,' she said. 'But I'm sure he is. Shall I pick him up?'

'Good lord, no, you got here first,' he laughed.

He took a deep breath. 'Lovely evening,' he said. 'Mark loves to come out on the green, my son, that is.'

'Yes, he told me. Also that he was almost six.'

'Yes, it's his birthday at the weekend. So you live in Cypress Grove?'

'Yes, over the dress shop,' she said.

'We've recently moved down from London, to Akers Green,' he said. 'It's about a mile away.'

'Oh, rather nice. Do you work locally?'

'I do now,' he said. 'Cirencester, I asked for a transfer and was lucky enough to get it.'

'So, quite handy,' she said, wondering what he did.

'I'm an architect,' he said.

And your wife, or partner, she wanted to ask.

'You might know my mother, Mark's grandmother,' he said. 'She runs the charity shop across from you – Dot Turnbull?'

'Oh, of course I do. I sometimes take the odd thing in there,' Genella said, and recalled some months ago hearing that her son's wife had died – how awful – but never thinking she would meet him.

'She's wonderful,' she laughed. 'Rules the helpers with a rod of iron.'

'She's a marvellous mother, too,' he said, looking in front of him. 'We called in to see her earlier.' There was a silence. 'I lost my wife, a year ago.'

'I'm sorry,' Genella said.

They were silent for a time. What a dreadful thing to happen, Genella thought, and the little boy, motherless.

'We were living in London but I have a good woman to look after him when I am at the office but, well, I'm not

90

making excuses, but I thought the country would be better for him. I grew up here and I loved it. He can see his gran sometimes or she might babysit. Altogether, it seems to be working out well.'

And now, Genella thought, you come to sit on the village green, back where you were born, where you belonged. And the little boy? Breathless and rosy cheeked, little Mark ran towards them. 'Can we go now?' he asked.

'Yes,' George said, standing up.

'Goodnight,' the boy said, and bent down to kiss and little dog. 'You be good,' and, looking very important, he took his father's hand.

'I hope we shall meet again,' George said. 'Goodnight.'

'Goodnight,' Genella said.

Oh, I do hope so, Genella thought. I do hope so.

It was quite late when Dot Turnbull locked up the charity-shop door; there was always plenty to do after closing time. She planned to pop in to Lamb Cottage for a moment to see her old friend Granny Holden. Granny Holden was a friend of long standing; had been, in fact, her own mother's friend. Had her mother lived they would have been about the same age.

She walked along the High Street, the street she knew so well, every inch of it, making a mental note of what was in the windows, until she came to the green, where on the corner, Granny Holden lived.

She knocked and called, 'Cooee, cooee, it's only me – it's Dot,' before the door was opened by the elderly lady who looked as if she had been crying.

'Whatever is it?' Dot said, closing the door firmly and putting an arm around the old lady.

'I've had a letter – from America,' she said. 'From Carol.'

'Oh, my, dear, you haven't!' Dot said. 'But that's good, isn't it?'

They sat down in the tiny sitting room.

'She's coming over – she and her husband—'

'Oh!' Dot said. 'Did you know she was married?'

''Course not!' Granny Holden said. 'When do I ever hear from her? The last time, oh, never mind . . . Oh, Dot, what am I to do? I feel the shock would kill me and what about Bernice?'

'She hasn't seen her since she was about five, has she?'

'And doesn't want to, she always says.'

'But where will she stay?' Dot asked, looking round. 'She can't stay here.'

'No, that's the point. 'They've booked in at The Old Manor House Hotel,' she said.

'Oh, my God!' Dot said. 'Bernice will be the first person she sees when she arrives.'

'In her letter, Carol says don't tell Bernice, she wants to surprise her.'

'Oh, that's cruel!' Dot said. 'The shock could kill her.'

'Well, she's tougher than that. But I, I'll have to think about it, Dot. I only got the letter today.'

'She didn't give you much notice, did she? When does she arrive?'

'This weekend, Sunday,' Granny Holden said.

They were silent for about five minutes. 'I'll put the kettle on,' Dot said.

Chapter Ten

Tony Sheridan lay on the bed, his arms behind his head, working out his plan of campaign, that is if indeed he had one, for he realised he had left a lot to chance where the jewellery was concerned. And not forgetting the little picture up on the wall, which fascinated him. And until he saw it closely, he would never know for sure if it was genuine. And how was he going to do that?

Putting aside all his aspirations, he got up and showered, thinking all the while as he did so. He would go to Lucknow Grange this time on his own. After all, he had made an appointment to see over it and, since it was not far away, near Stow, he would make a day of it.

He knew the girl, Ellis, would be on her own, for her mother was at their home at Charter Hall and would not be back until late. Well, that was not his problem, he would skip breakfast and have coffee and something to eat on the way. There was nothing quite as nice as driving round the countryside with not a thing to do, after all, his life was somewhat hectic in London.

His appointment was at eleven-thirty and, stopping at a small hotel just outside Stow, he had breakfast, charmingly served by a little waitress who eyed him with unconcealed admiration, but he was used to that. He made a note to patronise the hotel for an evening meal, should the occasion arise.

He arrived at Lucknow Grange at ten to eleven, having read through the particulars again on the brochure, and nearing it, he had to admit it certainly lived up to its description.

Once owned by a governor-general of India, hence the name, it stood out in all its glory in the lush countryside. Surrounded by fields, but enclosed by high iron railings, the approach was magnificent; great trees along the drive, while the building itself was obviously Georgian and built of Cotswold stone with magnificent windows and façade. He looked forward to seeing inside.

The agent greeted him, there being no one in charge except a housekeeper and a handyman, who retired to the kitchen.

What a pity, he thought, that this is all a game of pretence, for the house is everything a man would want. Gracious; a wonderful atmosphere; money had been spent on the bathrooms and kitchen area; it had a fine basement which could be used for a recreation room, and was a haven of rest in a topsy-turvy world.

He told himself he would give much to buy this house although, not having the wherewithal, it was out of the question. Besides, what would he do living out here in the middle of nowhere?

But beyond lay the fields with sheep roaming and the distant hills – he was quite carried away, for once in his life.

The agent knew when he had a client who was interested and began to outline the glories of the house, but Tony stopped him with the charm that only he knew how to use.

Once back in the hall, the agent, who thought he had a certain sale, stood with him, both admiring the walls, the ceiling, the furniture ...

'Well, sir,' he said encouragingly.

'I love it,' Tony said spontaneously. 'Undoubtedly,' he confided, 'I should have to see it again, and again, I daresay, since my fiancée—'

'Of course,' the agent murmured.

Tony looked at his watch, as if that helped. 'She will be back from Scotland in a couple of days – and we shall have to wait until then.'

'Could I say then, sir, that you are definitely interested?'

'Undoubtedly,' Tony said decidedly. 'That is, for my part, I cannot speak for her. How would it be?' he continued charmingly, 'if I get in touch with you in a couple of days? I'll fax you, and we'll ...' he left the rest of the sentence unfinished and looked again at his watch. 'Thank you so much for showing me around,' he looked back at the house again. 'Delightful,' he said softly, 'delightful.'

Well, it was, he thought as he drove away – pity it was all a game of make believe.

He stopped for a sandwich and a glass of wine before going on his way back to Cypress Grove.

The receptionist greeted him on his return. 'Did you manage to find it all right, Mr Sheridan?' Bernice asked.

'Yes, no trouble at all,' and he gave her a charming smile. 'Great,' he said. 'I quite enjoyed it. By the way, any messages?'

Phyllida consulted the noticeboard. 'No, not so far.'

'Thank you.' And he was away.

'I think he's really dishy,' Phyllida said. 'Don't you?'

'If you like the type,' Bernice said.

Sometimes Phyllida thought Bernice was a bit of a misery.

On his way back to his room, Tony used the stairs. It was a wide staircase, curving at the top, with a central stair carpet on a polished hardwood floor. The next flight consisted of five more stairs but it was at the top of the first part of the staircase on the side wall, out of his reach, that the little picture sat.

But it was was the one at the top that Tony was interested in – and still was – the more he saw of it. He stood briefly, eyeing it. He was as sure as he could be now that

95

the picture was a genuine miniature self portrait of Dudemeyer. The picture itself was quite small, about seven inches by five, and the frame was in slim brass with a ring at the top with which to hang. Unusual for a original painting to be framed, and yet . . .

If he wanted to examine it closely, night time would be better, although the lights were kept on throughout the hotel. He would have to think about it. But without seeing it close to he would never know if it was the genuine article.

Four thirty-five – he was not an afternoon-tea man, he would rest and get his thoughts together, shower and go down for an early drink.

So far he had wasted his time and the hotel was not cheap. But you never knew what was going to turn up and he was by nature an optimist.

He consulted his diary for the next few days and saw, almost with a shock, that the next day – the twenty-ninth – was his birthday, his fortieth.

He had known it was the coming weekend. But nowadays birthdays were not that important, not like when you were small and the family made a lot of it.

He supposed waiting back in London would be cards and perhaps a present of two. He wasn't close to his family, his brother and his sister – they had lost touch years ago, but his mother still remembered even if his father chose to cut him off.

Now, tomorrow, Saturday, and what was he going to do about the Macready jewels?

Ridiculous idea – the old dear would have them with her, he was sure, but she wasn't there and, if she was going to a big do that evening, she would take them with her. She would never leave them in a house full of workmen and would carry them around in a jewellery box, which would be kept in the hotel safe. Not tonight though, and he wondered not for the first time, if he was on a wild goose chase – the painting, the jewels . . .

He put in a few telephone calls to contacts in London and

later showered at his leisure and dressed for the evening. He was tying his tie when the thought came to him – why not ask that extraordinary girl – what was her name? Ellis – out to dinner this evening? Not in the hotel – that would set the tongues wagging – but at the little hotel he had been to this morning.

Not usually a creature of impulse, nevertheless, he rang reception and asked to be put through to Miss Macready's room.

He imagined the two receptionists eyeing each other but he couldn't help that.

'Hi, there,' a voice said, which was undoubtedly Ellis's.

'Ellis?'

'Yes, who is this?'

'Tony, Tony Sheridan,' he said. 'I hope I didn't disturb you?'

There was no answer.

'I wondered if you would have dinner with me this evening?'

'Oh! No, thank you, I—'

'I thought not in the hotel, somewhere private—'

'You don't wish to be seen with me?' she asked but he knew she was smiling.

'For lots of reasons,' he said. 'And I found a nice little place in a village.'

'Where?'

'Just outside Stow,' he said.

'I think I know it.'

'Well? If you'd rather not ...'

'Why not?' she asked. 'Are we celebrating something?'

'As a matter of fact, it's my birthday tomorrow,' he said.

She didn't say a word at this, obviously not believing him. 'Sure,' she said. 'I'll come. Wouldn't want you to be alone on your birthday eve.'

'Meet you in the foyer at seven and I'll book the table.'

'Sure,' she said. 'Thanks.' And that was that.

I must be mad he told himself.

Waiting in the foyer for her later, he saw the arrival of an elderly man, very well dressed, and a giggling young couple, the girl still with a sprinkle of confetti in her hair, before seeing Ellis come down the stairs wearing high heels and make up.

To say he was surprised was to say the least, for she looked quite different. Her long dress was simple but she carried a colourful shawl. She teetered towards him, her mascared eyes glowing, her lipstick carefully applied.

The strange thing was, he wasn't sure if he approved of the change ... He led her towards the exit, where they had brought his car round for him. Sitting in the driving seat, he turned to her and frowned.

'You don't approve of the new me,' she said.

'I liked the old one better,' he said and wondered why this was. He supposed she was quite attractive with her make up – and yet – she had lost something – something that made her different from other girls.

'You are a very rude man,' she said. 'You should be gracious and complimentary.' But she didn't look annoyed.

'It really is your birthday?'

'Why, did you think I was joking?'

'Well, I didn't believe you, that's for sure.'

The scent, though, was still delicious, and he wondered what it was.

They had little to say on the journey, which was not long, for they soon arrived at The True Lovers' Knot, which was more of a public house than an hotel.

'Very romantic,' she said. 'Yes, I do know it.'

'Been here before, have you?' he asked, locking the car.

'Yes, a long time ago, when we first moved to Charter Hall,' she said.

A waiter showed them to a corner seat and, once she was settled, gave them menus. They opted for asparagus followed by Dover sole and a good white wine.

'So, tell me how you got on looking over the other house. Where was it?'

'Lucknow Grange, charming, but not for me,' he said.

'You are proving very difficult to please,' Ellis said.

'I have only seen two.'

'I get the impression your heart isn't in it,' she said. 'Is there a woman in your life who has to be considered?'

The waiter brought their first course.

'No, not at all,' And he smiled. 'Of course, I cannot speak for the future.'

Ellis speared the wonderfully cooked vegetable. 'So, the decision has to be yours.'

'In the meantime,' Tony said. 'How did you get on at Charter Hall? Had they made any improvements?'

'Yes, quite a few, it's looking great.'

'Your mother must be pleased.'

'You must come over and see it sometime. Oh, I forgot, you are only here for a few more days.'

He wondered how she knew that. Had he mentioned leaving the following week? 'Yes, well, sometime; I should like that. Where do you live in America?' he asked.

'Mainly in New York but we have a country residence in Connecticut. My mother came from Minesota but my father was English.'

'Really?' he said. 'What did he do – your father?' As if he didn't know . . .

'He was a jeweller,' she said. 'Born in London, where his parents had a business, in Hatton Garden, and as a young man he opened up in New York, where he met my mother.'

'And you are an only child,' he said, savouring all this information.

'Yes, to their great regret. They would have liked a son, or sons, but—'

'I expect he adored you,' and his eyes looked into hers with true sincerity.

'Yes, he did spoil me, except for Johnnie.'

'Can't you imagine how upset he must have been? Such hopes, for you, I expect.'

'Well, he wasn't going to spoil me to the extent of giving me what I wanted,' she said.

And she's still smarting about it, he thought.

He felt a slight kick on his shin, and, looking down, saw that she had kicked off her high-heeled shoes. 'You are a nutcase,' he said.

'Is that bad?' she smiled.

She hasn't an ounce of coquetry in her, he decided. She doesn't even know how to flirt.

They took time eating the fish, which was excellent and fresh, then sat back to relax, she to wonder what her mother would think if she saw her now, and Tony to wonder what on earth this Johnnie had that made him so special.

Dessert seemed out of the question, so they had cheese, and finished up in the small friendly lounge for coffee.

By now she had her shoes on again and disappeared to the ladies room. When she returned, she was minus make up, and he saw the old Ellis. He smiled broadly.

'That better?' she said. 'I must say I do hate wearing it. Has it left black smudges?'

'No,' he said. Rarely had he enjoyed a woman's company more.

Now, fresh faced, she looked at him. 'What do you do?' she asked.

He was almost startled by the question. 'Do? Oh, finance mostly,' he said.

'Like working in a bank?'

'Oh dear me, no,' he said. 'That wouldn't suit me at all. I am a freelance financial adviser, I suppose you'd say. I work quite long hours – so I am glad of the holiday.'

'And you've made enough money to buy one of these splendid Cotswold houses?'

'Well,' he said, 'I hope so.'

'Have you had many – I was going to say affairs, but I mean marriages or broken engagements?'

For the first time he felt embarrassed. 'No, I've escaped, fairly reasonably,' he said.

'I can't think why,' she said.

She was slightly disturbing in that you never knew what she was going to ask next. 'You are very unusual,' he said. 'In this day and age.'

'So are you,' she said.

'In what way?'

'Well, handsome as all get out, rich, powerful, I presume – and unnattached.'

'I obviously don't suit the average young woman,' he said.

She glanced at her watch. 'Do you mind if we go now?'

'Not at all. Do you have to be back?'

'Mother is due back tonight – though late – and I want to be there for her. She might worry if I am not.'

'Of course you do,' he said, picking up her shawl and nodding to the waiter for the bill.

Outside, she stood breathing in the scented air. 'Let's walk through the garden. Just look at all these wonderful flowers – there is nothing like an English garden.'

He strolled with her, past the lights and the few people sitting on chairs.

They were silent going home, digesting what information the other had given. When they reached the hotel, she stood at the bottom of the stairs and held out her hand.

'Thank you, Tony,' she said. 'It was great.'

'Thank *you*,' he said.

Somehow, there was no thought of giving her a swift kiss but he knew he had enjoyed the evening, however unusual it had been.

When Mary-Ann returned, she had obviously had a wonderful evening. She looked magnificent in a ruby-red dress which fitted her slim figure and she wore brilliant rubies and earrings to match.

'What a wonderful evening!' she cried. 'And the people that were there – quite a few famous names – celebrities, and the speeches – I tell you, honey, Oxford does these things so well.'

'Let me help you,' Ellis said, and unclipped the necklace

while Mary-Ann took off the earrings.

'What did you do, darling?' she asked. 'Anything nice?'

'I went to a pub, with—'

'A pub?'

'Well, a small hotel, really, you'd know it.'

'With whom?' and she was serious, her evening forgotten.

'Tony Sheridan,' Ellis said casually.

And Mary-Ann's eyes sparkled. 'Oh, did you! Well done, how was it?'

'Great!'

'I should leave you alone more often,' Mary-Ann said, putting the jewellery away in the special casket.

'Ask the boy to come and take it down, will you dear,' she said, and she left for the bathroom.

'I'll do it,' Ellis said, picking up the little key. 'I want to post a letter off to the States and I want it to catch the first post in the morning.'

'Thank you, dear,' And, humming a little song, Mary-Ann disappeared into the bathroom.

A letter was put through Genella Hastings's front door late that night. It was from George Turnbull.

Dear Genella
Mark is having some friends to tea on Saturday and he
said he would like you to come.
At least, he said, 'the pretty lady with the little dog'.
Hope you can make it.
George

And he gave his address in Akers Green . . .

Chapter Eleven

Tony Sheridan had ostensibly been for a country walk.

He was dressed immaculately in tweeds, and a cap, every inch the country gentleman, using his walking stick to great effect and making his way back to the hotel.

It was a Saturday morning and his birthday, although he had forgotten it and, arriving back at the hotel, he made for the terrace where he ordered coffee. He was soon joined by Ellis Macready, who wished him a happy birthday and thanked him for the evening before.

When the waiter brought the coffee, she refused one, saying she was going out in half an hour with her mother to Cirencester.

Tony was not sure whether he was pleased with that or not, for she made a good companion, but he had things to do.

Idly, they watched as an elderly gentleman sat and ordered coffee and Ellis recognised him as the new arrival from the evening before.

James Elliott and Sybil and Kath sat over in the far corner, Sybil looking cross, but on seeing them Kath waved.

'I foresee some news in that direction before the week is out.' Tony grinned.

'What do you mean?' Ellis asked 'What sort of news?'

'Wait and see, and he smiled.

'Look,' Ellis said, seeing the pot of coffee in front of him. 'Leave that for a minute and come back and finish it later. I have something to show you.'

Mystified, Tony got to his feet, while Ellis went over to the waiter who was standing awaiting orders in the shady porch.

'Mr Sheridan will be back for his coffee, he won't be a moment,' she said and walked off through the flower garden, Tony following her.

When they had passed all the people looking or sitting in the gardens, Ellis sat down on the seat farthest away and motioned to Tony to sit down beside her.

He decided silence was the best policy and waited as she withdrew from her handbag a small silk bag, inside which was a narrow leather purse.

'This is for you,' she said. 'Happy birthday!'

Mystified, he opened the purse and saw inside a man's tiepin – something he hadn't seen for years. 'What—' he began.

'I know men don't wear them nowadays but it's for you. It belonged to my father and I want you to have it.'

The tiepin was of gold and at the top sat a single solitaire diamond of goodness knows how many carats.

He took a sharp intake of breath. 'What's this for? I can't take this, Ellis!'

But she was serene and sure. 'It is for making me welcome and taking me out. You made me feel like a person again,' she said.

'Taking you out!' he repeated. 'To that poor little hotel?'

'I loved it,' she said sincerely. 'The last few days I feel I have got back – well, a little – of my self esteem.'

God, what must the past have been like, he wondered.

He leaned forward and kissed her lightly on the cheek. 'You're very sweet, Ellis, but I can't take it, my dear. I can see it's worth a fortune.'

She flushed. 'I mean it, Tony. It is mine, my father left

it to me and I would rather you have it – than anyone.'

What would her mother say? he asked himself. Of course he wanted it. It must be worth a great deal. Still, regretfully . . .

'I mean it,' she said, showing the adamant side of her nature again. 'I want you to have it,' and she got to her feet. 'I must fly, Mother will be waiting.'

And he was left, sitting there with the diamond pin winking at him in the sun.

We walked back slowly to his table, noticing gratefully that his umbrella was still there – and the coffee pot. The waiter hovered suggesting that he bring fresh coffee and Tony assented.

He sat thinking, while the talk went on all around him. What a turn up for the book! Still, he couldn't take it. When Mary-Ann found out she would be livid.

It obviously satisfied something in the girl's make up and in truth they had got on together in a sort of way. He had thought at the time that she had been delighted to be asked to see the house. Who knew what a girl in her situation would be thinking? It was a first for him. It was usually the other way round.

Constance came over to say hello. She was a nice woman. Friendly, but not pushingly so. He knew she had recently retired, and had been PA to someone. That job would suit her.

Finishing his coffee, he made tracks towards the hotel itself, past the two receptionists, who smiled at him, making for the stairs, and taking them slowly as he glanced once more towards the small picture. That's what this was all about – now he needed the walking stick.

Once in his room he locked the door and took out the little purse. No, he had not been dreaming – it was there – still, and he decided for safety to keep it on his person. He stuffed it in the top pocket of his sports jacket – for now, and got down to the business he had been planning the whole morning.

From his trouser pocket he withdrew a packet of cup hooks that he had purchased at the hardware shop in the village, where he had also bought the umbrella in the tailors.

Examining the bottom of the walking stick, he realised it would be quite difficult to insert a screw. The handle itself was far too thick to curve round a small nail. He imagined the clutter if the small picture fell to the wooden floor. The wood of the stick was brick hard, ash probably, with the need to be sturdy. But he wouldn't give up. This was the only way he could see clearly to getting that damn picture off the wall.

An hour later, he had, with the aid of a sharp penknife, made a tiny incision in the base of the stick, then came the effort of trying to insert the screw. You're losing your grip, Tony he told himself. You should have bought a bradawl. He had been called on to do all sorts of things in his time.

Now the screw was safely inserted in the walking stick, and heaving a sigh of relief, he hung it in the wardrobe and, washing his hands, began to get ready for lunch.

It being Saturday, Constance decided to have a pre-lunch drink. After all, this time next week, she would be on her way home. A gin and tonic, in the lounge – that was the idea. She felt almost reckless.

Sitting in the bar like any other sophisticate, she thought again what a splendid hotel this was. Run on oiled wheels, one hardly every saw the owners, for she had heard it was privately owned. She had seen through reception once to the office where a handsome middle-aged woman, well dressed, had her back to her. That would be Mrs Markham, she guessed, while her husband made fleeting appearances from time to time.

I wouldn't mind that, she mused, running an hotel. But she quickly realised she was the sort of woman who got swept away with things she was not used to – like living in a cottage on the green. Oh, dear me no. But she had been keen at the time. Keen enough to go to the estate agent, which reminded her, she had just seen Tony Sheridan and wondered how far he had got in his house hunting. I am a creature of impulse, she told herself, but as long as I keep one foot on the ground ... Then she saw the elderly man enter the bar with his paper under his arm. Going up to the bar, he ordered and took his seat at the next table.

Strangely, there was something slightly familiar about him, as if she had seen him before, but that wasn't likely. As if he read her thoughts, he turned and held out a hand.

'John Stansbridge,' he said as the waiter arrived at that moment with the drink.

'Constance Boswell,' she said.

'May I join you?'

'Please do,' she smiled, and blushed at the same time.

At this age she should have grown out of that ridiculous habit. A doctor had once told her it was quite common with a lot of women but would lessen as she got older.

He looked at her. 'I hope you don't think I am excessively rude,' he said, 'but I get the impression I have seen you before.'

She wasn't going to admit she thought so too.

'Do you come from London?'

'Yes, I've recently retired from the City,' she said, and thought how the world had changed. It seemed quite natural now to talk to strangers without a proper introduction.

'Ah! That's it then, I too have worked in the City, well, all my life,' he said. 'Our paths may have crossed at some time.'

The waiter returned. 'Excuse me, Sir John, there is a telephone call for you, if you would follow me,' he said, and the man did so.

Sir John Stansbridge! Of course, their paths had crossed many times, impersonally, at City meetings, he was a City councillor and probably knew Joe.

He returned quite shortly, apologising.

'It doesn't matter where you go, business follows,' he smiled, taking his seat.

'You are taking a well-earned holiday, I am sure,' she said.

'No, not quite, I have retired recently, three months ago, and promised myself this short holiday before I go to the States to visit my daughter, who lives there.'

'Ah,' she smiled, wondering about his wife.

'You are not married?' he asked.

'No, I have never been married,' Constance said, 'but I have worked in the City all my life.'

'May I ask where you worked?'

'In Maxwell's paper merchants, in St Mary Axe.'

He smiled. 'Oh, I know it well. An old established firm. I hear Joe Maxwell is on the point of retiring, too.'

Well, she didn't know that. This man and Joe would be about the same age, sixty-five. It was annoying, though, to find someone out of her own private world. It was as if she was being spied on. But he was nice man, good company.

'Are you on your own here?' he asked.

Pointed question, she thought.

'Yes, I am,' she said coolly. What business was it of his?

'Perhaps you would have dinner with me this evening, unless you are doing anything. We could talk of old times, in the City?'

It was on the tip of Constance's tongue to refuse but then she changed her mind. Why not? They had at least something in common. She smiled. 'I should like that,' she said.

Having bought a book and a toy tractor for the small boy Mark on his birthday, and after closing the shop, Genella Hastings made her way out of Cypress Grove towards Akers Green. It was less than two miles away and she was there in no time. The cottage, White Cottage, was in the village High Street, surrounded by trees and shrubs. There was a white wooden gate, with a red balloon on top, and Genella pulled in to the driveway.

Such a pretty little house. She felt quite envious. How nice of George to ask her although apparently it was Mark's idea. Who would have imagined this time last week she would be going to a small boy's birthday party?

Dot Turnbull opened the door to her, obviously pleased to see her. 'Oh, Genella, I am glad you came. You look lovely, dear.'

Genella was pleased. She had made an effort not to over-dress but to put something pretty on.

The noise coming from the back garden certainly indicated a party and Dot led the way through the cottage to the garden outside, where there were four small boys and one little girl.

'He doesn't know many children yet,' Dot whispered, 'but six is enough, believe me.'

George upended himself from a garden seat and came towards her. 'I'm glad you came, that you found the time,' he said.

'I wouldn't have missed it for the world,' Genella said, and thought, when did I last, at least, since I've been a grown up, ever go to a children's birthday party?

But it was a lovely atmosphere – one that she was not used to.

Little Mark came up to her and was as pleased as punch with his presents but disappointed at the same time. 'You didn't bring your little dog, Charlie,' he said. 'Doesn't he like parties?'

'I don't know,' she said slowly. 'I don't think he has ever been to one and I wasn't sure he would behave.'

'We would have looked after him,' he said reproachfully. 'P'raps I'll see him on the green again.'

'I am sure you will,' she said. 'I hope so.'

As George came towards her with an iced drink, he smiled at her, such a warm friendly smile. She decided she liked this man – Dot Turnbull's son – and spared a thought for the mother of the little boy, who was not here today.

She smiled back at him and held out her hand for the drink.

'Thank you, George,' she said. 'And thank you for inviting me. You have a very pretty house here.'

'Yes, I think we did rather well. Do sit down and make yourself at home.'

If only, she thought wistfully . . .

The hotel was quiet at almost three in the morning but Tony Sheridan was still awake. In fact, he hadn't gone to bed; he was listening for any sounds of activity outside in the corridor and on the stairs. Once opening his door, he saw that it was deathly still outside and, although all the lights were on, they were dimmed.

The longer he put it off, the worse it would become, so, as silently as a mouse, he took out the stick from the wardrobe, and made for the door.

His heart was beating rapidly, but he enjoyed this kind of situation. Loved the thrill of it, the excitement and, walking along to the bend in the stairs, held out the stick towards the picture. He had been right about the height. The hook easily lifted off the little picture, leaving the nail bare and the spare space seemed to him to stand out a mile. But it was above the average person's head and he couldn't see in the half light whether or not it had left a mark.

He stowd the picture in his pocket and crept back to his room, locking the door behind him. Heart beating uncomfortably, he stared down at the little framed picture in his hand. He turned it over. That was the important part but there was no signature and he examined it under his magnifying glass to no avail.

Presently he prised open the frame and eased out the painting, excited beyond measure as to what he would see.

110

It was an original painting all right, and of Dudemeyer. But had he painted it?

Study it as he would under his magnifying glass, he was not sure. Under the glare of his torch he was still not sure. He put a damp finger on it gently, fingered it, the edges – then sat back.

He knew from the history of this house, that the original owners, the Ashbys, had had a fine collection of paintings, mostly originals.

Some were sold when the house was turned into a hotel, and some were kept. Because they added distinction to such a place, many were replaced by copies but was this one? The hell of if was he was not sure. Painted by the master it would be worth a fortune – a copy, nothing.

He flopped down on the bed, his mind a maelstrom of thoughts. He was on a wild-goose chase – and not for the first time.

But his gut feeling might be right. Suppose it was. Well, there was only one man he knew who could answer his question – Bertrand Meyer, a Dutchman, with premises in London. He had an art gallery in Poland Street and lived over the shop. He would have to go up and see him and the sooner the better.

Would he be there on a Sunday? He had no time to waste. First thing in the morning he would give him a call – but not from the hotel. He would leave, by car, as reasonably early as he could and drive to London, assuming Meyer would be in, phone him on the way.

That was the only way he was going to get an answer.

It had been a long day – Saturdays always were and the Markhams were ready for bed.

Sunday would be easier, except for lunch, which was mostly the chef's and the kitchen's responsibility.

'So, the Americans arrive tomorrow,' Grace said.

'Yes, mid morning in time for lunch, I expect,' Robert said.

'We had another call today from California but I had to explain that we were fully booked until September, so they booked for then.'

'Good,' Robert said, and went off into the bathroom.

Chapter Twelve

On Saturday evening after her little grandson's party, Dot Turnbull hurried along to see her friend, Granny Holden. She was worried about her; knew that she was fearful of the visit of her long-lost daughter the next day, dreaded it in fact.

She wouldn't stay long – just long enough to have a cup of tea and see her to bed. Goodness knows what Bernice would do – it didn't bear thinking of.

She found Granny Holden sitting quietly watching television, which she switched off as soon as Dot let herself in with her own key.

'Don't do that – I'm only here for a minute.'

She went over and kissed the old lady who was quite flushed.

'Oh, there's nothing on, Saturdays, is there?' she said in disgust. 'I'm glad to see you, Dot. How did the party go?'

'Well, very well. They all had a lovely time and I must say I enjoyed it. Genella came – you know the dress-shop lady?'

'Genella? What was she doing there?'

'George and young Mark met her walking her dog on the green. Mark was very impressed, and asked her to the party.'

'And she came?'

'Yes, and what's more seemed to enjoy herself. Mind

you, I think Mark expected her to bring the dog,' and she laughed.

'Well, divorced and no children. Who knows what her life is like after the shop closes? She probably gets very lonely.'

'I must say, George seemed to like her a lot. Wouldn't it be great if—'

'Now, Dot, don't count your chickens,' and she laughed.

Dot laughed with her. 'Now, what about you?'

'I hope I get a good night's sleep, don't want to lie awake tossing and turning.'

'No, because there is nothing you can do about it at this stage of the game. Now, they're coming to tea in the afternoon, aren't they and Bernice will be home for lunch?'

'Oh!' Gran gave a heavy sign.

'I just wish Carol hadn't asked me not to say anything. Think what Bernice will feel like coming face to face with her mother after all these years.'

'Yes, well, she must have had her reasons. Now, if you're sure you'll be all right, I'll pop off now and I'll call in after church, have a quick cuppa with you.'

'You are good, Dot,' Granny Holden said as Dot let herself out.

The next morning Dot called in, to find roast beef in the oven, roast potatoes cooking nicely and a Yorkshire pudding ready to go in. There were raspberries for afterwards picked from the garden. Dot knew she adored this granddaughter of hers and hoped and prayed nothing would happen to destroy the special relationship they had.

When she had gone, Granny Holden took out Carol's letter again and read it for the hundredth time.

It wouldn't be long now.

The Warburgs arrived around midday at The Old Manor House in the hired limousine from Heathrow.

The chauffeur took their cases from the boot and was

114

greeted by Tom Reading, the uniformed attendant, who welcomed them to the hotel. As he bent to pick up the cases, Carol Warburg looked hard at him.

'Don't I know you?' she asked, her American accent unmistakable. 'I went to school with you, didn't I?' But she sounded puzzled.

'I expect it was my father,' Tom grinned. 'John Reading.' He was about to say, 'He is around the same age as yourself' but forbore to say so.

'John Reading!' she said. 'Of course.' She held out her hand.

'I'm Carol Warburg. I was born here, went to school here.' Dwight Warburg stood by. He was used to his wife's impulsive actions.

Tom picked up the two suitcases. 'Welcome to The Old Manor House,' he said. 'I hope you have a very pleasant stay.' He moved through to the reception areas towards the stairs.

At the desk Carol stood and looked around.

'I used to work here, for a short time,' she said, looking hard at the two receptionists.

Dwight Warburg busied himself with booking in. He hadn't approved of this whole idea, but after two years of marriage, was used to his wife's idiosyncrasies and, since all he wanted was to please her, he had given in.

Robert Markham appeared as if from nowhere, obviously if not the owner, then the man in charge.

They shook hands. 'Mr Warburg,' he said, 'Mrs Warburg, welcome to The Old Manor House. I hope you will enjoy your stay.'

Carol Warburg wore large dary glasses, so that it was impossible to see what was going on behind them. She was about sixty and extremely attractive with short blonde hair, very stylishly cut, although it was easy to see she was born a brunette. She wore a trouser suit in pale grey, both receptionists noted the Louis Vuitton luggage and her handbag. She looked from one to the other of them.

115

They were warm in their welcome and the visitors signed the register and, at the end of the short discussion with Robert Markham, understood they were to be given Apartment Two, which was the best in the hotel.

Young Ronnie, who assisted Tom at weekends took the smaller cases and waited for them to follow to the lift.

'Well, I'll be off.' Bernice said. 'See you tomorrow, Phyll.' And collecting her handbag walked the short distance to Lamb Cottage.

In the luxurious apartment Dwight Warburg looked round appreciatively.

'Nice room,' he said and, looking out of the window to the garden area, whistled approvingly.

'This is great.' He turned to see Carol sitting on the edge of the bed, dabbing a hankie to her eyes.

'Oh, I wish I hadn't come!' she said.

'Now, sweetie,' he said. 'You've been on about this trip for the past six months. What's wrong? Are you disappointed?'

She shook her head. 'No, of course not. It's just that I shouldn't have planned it like this.'

He couldn't agree more but that is what she had wanted.

'Which one,' he asked gently, 'is your daughter?'

'You couldn't tell?' she sounded amazed.

He shook his head.

'The one on the left – the pretty one,' she sniffed.

'She is not in the least like you,' he said.

'She's dark; I used to be,' she said.

She collapsed on to the bed. 'Oh, Dwight, my poor mother, how could I do this to her?'

'I've often wondered,' he said mildly. 'Look, you'll feel better when we're had a drink and some lunch.'

She got up from the bed. 'I don't know how I am going to go through with this.'

'Now, honey, you've been looking forward to this for

116

weeks. What's caused the change of mind?'

She shook her head. 'The reality of it all – what I'm doing – it seemed such a good idea at the time.'

'Yep, that often happens,' he said wryly. 'Well, use that excellent bathroom, wash your face, and we'll go down to lunch.'

In the bathroom she took off her glasses to expose large dark eyes, lovely eyes, normally soft and warm – most people noticed her eyes first.

I wonder what Mum will think of me now? she wondered. I left all those years ago, left her with little Bernice, who was five. I don't know now how I could have done it. And yet I *had* to do it. A few sporadic letters which ceased when I married my first husband. And that had been a catastrophe. Then another marriage, and a move farther north. Thank God she had had no more children. Another painful divorce, after which she took herself in hand, got a good job and eventually met Dwight, which was the best thing she had ever done.

She had wanted to come home and see her mother for years, but had not found the courage. Both her first two husbands had been against the idea, they wanted her past buried. And somehow she had worked out that a clean break with little Bernice was the best thing. She knew she was in her mother's capable hands – and should anything have happened to either of them she would have been home like a shot.

So, I'm not perfect, she told herself. She washed her face and cleaned her teeth, and applied fresh make up.

Feeling a little better, which Dwight was glad to see, she went over and kissed him. 'I'm sorry,' she said. 'After all you've done for me.'

'Well, how can you be down in a wonderful place like this? We're going to enjoy ourselves, aren't we?'

'Sure,' she said, though trembling lips.

This afternoon, she thought, I must go on my own.

Dwight can follow later – that's if it all works out all right. She would go about four, tea time in England.

Already, she had decided, she would say nothing about her discovery. Yes, she had found her father – that had been the first shock. With help from the Army authorities they had traced him in South Carolina.

She went there but didn't look him up immediately. She found out where he lived – of course, he was older. Married with three children – all boys. Married as soon as he got back from the war. She had seen the marriage certificate. She judged he had left an engaged girl behind him.

She drove out to the farm where he lived and sat in the car for a long time then took herself back to her hotel, wondering what he would say if he knew that his daughter from England was staying just down the road from him.

That night she had cried herself to sleep. Even regretting that she had found him. What, she wondered, would his reaction be if he knew that she existed?

Her mother had received no notification of his death, no news of him at all. She was no relation to him. His family had welcomed him home and the celebrations were followed by a wedding. How awful it must have been, waiting day after day for news.

Carol saw him though. One day driving past the farm where he lived. There were three men standing together by the wide gates and they looked at her as she drove slowly past. She recognised him from the photograph her mother still kept in her bedroom. Farther on she stopped and wept as if her heart would break.

She made a vow then that she would never say a word. After all, this was Bernice's grandfather – but it made no sense. No one would thank her for digging up a bit of history and she had turned her back on South Carolina and written to her mother:

'No luck yet. Love Carol.'

118

And she would keep it that way.

Just before four o'clock, Carol got herself ready to go. She wore a skirt and top. She wondered how her mother would feel – when she had left all that time ago her hair had been dark and she would be shocked to see her as a blonde – still none of that mattered.

Dwight, who was reading the paper on the bed looked up as she stood beside him, ready to go.

'You look lovely,' he said and got to his feet and held her tightly. 'You can do it,' he said. 'Think how pleased your ma is going to be.'

He knew she was on the verge of more tears and gave her a little shove.

'Go on, get it over with and I'll be over there about six, OK?'

'Just cross over the road on to the green and—'

'Honey, I know where it is. I'll see you there about six. Good luck,' and he kissed her.

In a matter of minutes she stood outside the front door of Lamb Cottage, her heart beating like a wild thing. She rang the bell and suddenly the door opened and she was faced by a small, white-haired elderly lady she didn't recognise at first, but her arms went round the slight figure instinctively and she held her tightly. How small and frail she was oh, the shock for her . . . They seemed to stand like that for ages, until she eased herself away and they stood and looked at each other.

'I can't believe it,' said Granny Holden. 'That I should live to see this day. Come in.'

The house wasn't strange, after all, she had been born there and grew up there, although now it looked so tiny and different.

'You look wonderful,' Granny Holden said. 'My word, I wouldn't have known you, blonde eh?'

'Well, you try to keep young.' It sounded so banal.

'I liked your dark curls better.'

119

Carol looked around apprehensively. 'Where's ...
Bernice?'

'In the garden, reading. She usually sits out there
when she's off duty. You can relax, I haven't said a word.'

She saw at once that her mother was the stronger of them
both.

She bit her lip. 'I don't know if I am up to this, Mum,'
she said, and her voice trembled.

'It was your idea,' Granny Holden said. 'How do you
think I feel?'

She was still the strong woman she had always been,
Carol thought. Tiny though she was now, you could feel
her strength. God forgive me for staying away all these
years.

But now she must go through with it.

'What shall we have – a cup of tea?'

'Yes, put the kettle on, the table's laid and there's a cake
in the tin.'

Carol went over to the sink. 'Oh, what happened to the
range?'

'We have gas now,' Granny Holden said.

No thanks to you, she thought, and was surprised to feel
that underneath her joy at seeing her daughter again she felt
a shaft of bitterness go through her. She had never in her
wildest dreams imagined that she would see her daughter
again.

After the initial shock, she felt stronger. 'I'll call
Bernice,' she said, and heard Carol's slight intake of
breath.

'Bernice!' she called, 'tea's ready!'

Bernice closed her book and stood still for a moment
before going through the garden door to the kitchen.

She betrayed not by a look or gesture that she had seen
the woman before, just stood still, facing her.

'Bernice,' Granny Holden said, 'this is—'

'I know, we met this morning,' Bernice said.

Carol took a deep breath. 'What I want to say, and I

don't know how to say it, is that I am your mother.'

'I know,' Bernice said without the slightest interest.

Carol gasped. 'What do you mean – you know?'

'Shall we sit down?' Bernice said. Of the three of them, she was the most calm.

How cold she was! Carol felt in a state of shock.

Bernice put out a hand and covered her grandmother's. 'Gran, don't be upset, it's all been a shock but don't worry about me. As for you, and she turned to face Carol. 'Words fail me that you could so such a thing, after all this time.'

Carol was weeping now. 'I wanted to see you – both – again . . .'

'Pity you left it so long,' Bernice said. Her eyes were cold. 'I've known most of your movements for many years,' she said and turned to her grandmother.

'Do you remember Pat Hayley, who I went to school with? She went to America.'

'You still get letters from her – is that the one?'

'Yes, that's her. Well, when she first went, I asked her to find out – if she could – the whereabouts of my mother. I was keen to know then,' and she twisted her lip. 'She's been a great friend – she traced you several times, from your short visit to South Carolina to Richmond, Virginia, thence to Chicago and Boston and now New York. She herself got interested and she even hired a private detective for me that I paid for, so don't worry about that, Gran—'

'But why did you never tell me? Granny Holden said.

'I didn't want to upset you,' Bernice said.

'You went to South Carolina?' Granny Holden's eyes were wide. Did you?'

Carol sent an anguished appeal to Bernice and shook her head. 'No . . . no . . .'

'Best get on with your tea,' Bernice said. 'I'm going back to work – I'm on duty at six.'

'Oh, Bernice!' Carol cried but, without a backward look

121

at her mother, Bernice bent over and kissed her Granny Holden.

'Take it easy,' she said. 'Don't wait up for me, I'll be late.'

Chapter Thirteen

Tony Sheridan drove on this fine Sunday morning towards London, his mind full of the small picture in his briefcase. He would soon know for sure. Ringing on his mobile, he had found to his satisfaction that Bertrand Meyer was in residence at his flat in Poland Street and would be pleased to see him.

Parking was easier on a Sunday and he soon found space nearby, glancing in the gallery window to see what his friend had on display at the moment.

Yes, he was the man to put his mind to rest. He rang the doorbell and pushed the button to gain entrance.

The voice came back clearly. 'Come on up, Tony ...'

He pushed open the door and made for the steep stairs. After a week in the Cotswolds, London seemed overfull of people and noise and humidity.

The apartment was comfortably furnished, as it would be, Bertrand Meyer being an art connoisseur, and he greeted his friend warmly.

'Phew, it's warm isn't it?' he greeted him. 'So you've come up from the country. Lucky you – I could do with air conditioning in this place. Sit down, and let's see what you have.'

Tony felt he had come home. These were the surroundings he was used to.

'Coffee? Or would you rather get this over first?'

'First, please, old man,' Tony said, realising just how het up he was now that he was faced with reality.

'Let's see it then.'

Tony dived into his inner pocket and brought out the protected painting in its narrow brass frame.

It was was an elegant painting in sepia, a typical elderly Dutchman of the period: long curly grey hair, with a scarf round his head like a skull cap, and he was wearing a cloak with a fur collar. A head-and-shoulders portrait.

Not by a flicker did Meyer betray his thoughts at this stage, but took it and unwrapped it.

He looked over his glasses at Tony. 'I should warn you first that Dudemeyer was not into miniatures. But who knows?'

Tony watched every slight change of expression as Meyer peered at it, got out his magnifying glass, some other implements, and took it over to the window.

He kept silent as Meyer removed the picture from its surround and squinted yet again, felt it, turned it over. He felt the suspense building up inside him.

Presently Meyer laid it down on the table and shook his head. 'Sorry old man, but it's a copy. Well done, but a copy.'

He took it over to a small table on which stood a glass stand with a powerful light which he switched on, placing the picture beneath.

'Look yourself if you want to. But I doubt you'd see what I can see. Tiny impressions, all sorts of things. I don't say it set out to be a fake but is a genuine copy by someone who admired Dudemeyer and his work.'

He looked up at Tony. 'Sorry,' he said. 'It's a sod when that happens.'

'I really thought it was genuine,' Tony murmured.

'Well, you would – as an amateur. It might get past a lot of people – but not me.'

He did not underestimate his superiority. 'You could always get another opinion.'

But Tony smiled. 'That's not likely.'

Meyer switched off the machine. 'Have a drink,' he said. 'I'm sure you could do with one.'

'Please,' Tony said. He could not have been more disappointed.

'What's it worth?' he asked.

'Considering the subject – a hundred – fifty, whatever anyone likes to pay you for it – a fiver.'

'Thanks, mate,' Tony laughed.

Meyer went over to the drinks cabinet. 'Where did you find it?'

'I don't think it would help if I told you,' Tony said. 'And I'm not about to do that.'

'Fair enough. Got a fine painting by Dudemeyer if you are interested?'

'No thanks,' Tony laughed. 'Er, whisky please.'

'My pleasure,' Meyer said. 'Glad to have been of help.'

'Send me your bill,' Tony said.

'Same address?' Meyer asked.

After all, nobody did anything for nothing these days.

Back in the hotel, Tony glanced up the stairs – he was tempted to put the blasted thing back, but knew he couldn't.

He had looked through to the terrace, where several people were having drinks, but there was no sign of Ellis or her mother.

Constance was in close conversation with Sir John Whatisname while the two friends were still accompanied by James Elliott.

Bored, he went back to his room, to read through the Sunday newspapers. But he wasn't reading half the time – he was trying to assess the previous week and what had happened.

He got up and felt in the top pocket of his jacket. Yes, the tiepin was still there. Well, that was a turn up for the book and yes, he would keep it. Accept it graciously. After

125

all, she wanted him to have it – and it was worth a bob or two.

He fell to thinking about her and the possibilities in that direction. Jewellery there was, by all accounts, but how the devil to get hold of it?

Strangely enough, he found he had a soft spot for Ellis. Not his cup of tea at all – not in that way – but she was so different from the girls he usually met; she was almost refreshing.

That had been the reason for coming down here – the Macreadys and their jewellery – and if nothing else it had been a change from London.

Tonight he must get rid of the picture – the longer he held on to it the more dangerous it became when the loss was discovered.

Sir John and Constance Boswell were deep in conversation: talking of the City and how much it had changed over forty years.

'Our memories go back a long way,' Sir John said.

So far they had avoided any mention of Joe Maxwell and his family.

'To say nothing of the new underground. Whoever would have thought there would be a City airport?'

'And Canary Wharf, it's more like New York now than London.'

It was nice to have someone to talk to who knew your background Constance decided, but the more they talked of the City, the more she thought about Joe.

She had dreamt of him last night – the dream had been so real. It was of the times they had met covertly years ago and she woke up feeling quite disturbed.

Once awake, she went over their friendship, knowing that half of the trouble was because she missed the business. How could you spend forty years doing a certain job without having some feeling for it?

Then when her parents died, Joe had been so kind.

That's when it had all begun. He had found her the little flat in Clapham, although he never visited her there. Some people might say he had taken advantage of a young vulnerable girl, but it had been as much her fault as his.

Then the problem with his sons – at least with one of them. Got himself involved with an undesirable girl and Joe used to open his heart to her and tell her of his worries. His wife seemed to have no such qualms. Fortunately, it had all ended well. But it was hard to be part of a family and yet not be.

'So, what are you going to do with yourself when you get back to London?' Sir John was asking.

The sixty-four dollar question, Constance thought. Tomorrow was the start of her second week and, although she had enjoyed it, she was no nearer making any decisions.

After all, she didn't have to do anything. She had enough money to keep her self quietly – the odd holiday – as this one had been – not always so expensive, of course, but it had been worth every penny, for she had met so many interesting people.

She sighed. 'I don't know, Sir John.'

'Please call me John,' he said. 'You know, I was only knighted last year and it is still new to me.'

'And you are off to America to see your daughter. How exciting.'

'Yes, it is. She married an American two years ago – and they live in Boston. I've been there before, and liked it very much.'

Someone of his own, she thought. That's what she missed. But she brightened. Freedom – many would envy her.

Arriving back at The Old Manor House, Bernice had hung her jacket on its hanger and rejoined Phyllida at the reception desk.

'How is your Gran?' Phyllida asked. She was fond of

Granny Holden. Everyone liked her.

'Fine,' Bernice said, and decided to make a clean breast of it. Better now than later.

'Phyll, these people, Americans who came this morning.'

'The Warburgs?'

'Don't think I'm mad but I'd better tell you now – she is my mother, Mrs Warburg.'

Phyllida's mouth was open. 'You're joking! Your mother? What do you mean?'

'I'll make it short. She's come over to see my gran and to reintroduce herself to me.' There was no mistaking the sneer on her face.

'Bernice! That attractive American, is she really your mother?'

'Yes, the bleached one.' Her lip curled.

'Oh, hold on, I thought—'

'It doesn't matter what you thought. She was hoping to surprise me but she was unlucky, wasn't she?'

'What do you mean?'

Bernice took a deep breath. 'I'll make it brief – I knew about her. A friend of mine has been in touch all through the years and I knew who she was and where she was.'

Phyllida was shocked. 'Bernice! And you never said a word.'

'What to say?' Bernice asked. Her face was pale and she looked drawn as if she hadn't slept.

'I'm not exactly proud of the fact that she didn't want to know me.' Phyllida realised then just what her friend might have gone through over the years. She may have appeared hard and uncaring, but imagine what it must have meant to her. What an awful thing. No wonder . . .

She put out a hand, covered Bernice's. 'Anything I can do, you let me know,' she said, as a couple came in to retrieve their keys.

'Good evening, have you had a nice day?'

Business must go on.

*

'You've absolutely ruined this holiday,' Sybil stormed at Kath. 'Inviting that old man everywhere we go. Not a word about me.'

'Oh, don't start again!' Kath said. 'I don't know what you have against him. He's a dear old man.'

'There! You see! You admit it. He is an old man.'

'Well, you know what I mean, he's rather sweet, in his way.'

'Sweet! You want your head examining. I tell you Kath, this will be the last holiday I go on with you, if you're going to do this sort of thing.'

Kath was ominously quiet. 'What do you mean – "this sort of thing"?'

'Well, flirting.'

'Me? Flirting?'

'You know what I mean.'

'I'm afraid I don't.' Kath looked sulky.

'I wonder if he would be interested to know you have already had three husbands,' Sybil said mildly.

'That's typical of you,' Kath said bitterly. 'And you'd do it, wouldn't you, if you thought that would get rid of him?'

'I would indeed,' Sybil said smugly, and tried a bit of wheedling. 'Let's make the most of our few days, Kath. Go for an outing, get rid of the old bore.'

But she could see it would take a lot to bring Kath round.

Later that Sunday evening, Robert Markham greeted Tony Sheridan.

'Had a good day, Mr Sheridan?'

'Excellent,' Tony said, and made up his mind on the spur of the moment. 'I'm off to see another house tomorrow – perhaps I will be luckier this time.'

'It is not easy,' Robert Markham said seriously. 'Not an enviable task ... so many things to consider.'

'Exactly,' Tony said with his charming smile and, nodding to the two ladies, who seemed to be arguing, went over to the lift.

That settled his tomorrow then. He freshened up, and took out the pile of brochures he had received from the agents, and browsed through them.

Somerset Hall, he read. Little Bristow, why not? Perhaps if he saw Ellis again he would ask her to go with him. He had quite enjoyed her company on that first visit.

He knew he was putting off deciding what to do with the picture. Taking it out of his pocket, he cleaned and dusted it for fingerprints, slipping it inside a perfectly ordinary little plastic bag and placed it in his jacket pocket. Easy to dump it somewhere and, after a day in London, he felt like a walk.

Taking his walking stick out of the cupboard, he undid the screw at the base and put it in his toilet bag then, armed for an evening's country walk, he set off out of the hotel.

He made for the High Street, passing the shops on one side, and saw the attractive woman from the dress shop close her side door and come out with the little dog.

'Pleasant evening,' he said, and walked on. He came to the green, where there were several people, sauntering, and children playing with a ball. He walked on until he came to a copse. It was shady in the evening sun but he couldn't throw a walking stick there. It would be easily noticed. He was surprised how difficult it was to get rid of something when you wanted to. Besides, they might notice at reception that he hadn't got his stick with him. All these ridiculous thoughts went through his mind until he crossed over to the other side of the road and came to the charity shop.

There was a step down to the shop and two large black bins bags sat there. On the door was a notice: PLEASE DO NOT LEAVE DONATIONS WHEN THE SHOP IS CLOSED.

He stepped down, ostensibly peering through the glass door to see something the better, he already had the tiny packet out of his pocket, and it seemed to take but a moment before it was through the letter box and had fallen to the floor inside.

130

He stepped back to the window and peered at the various things hanging on the wall – no point in rushing now – the deed was done.

Presently, straightening himself up, he swung his stick along the pavement and around the corner, to The Old Manor House Hotel.

'Nice walk?' Phyllida asked with a warm smile. She thought Tony Sheridan was dishy and envied the American girl when she saw her going out with him.

'Very nice,' Tony said. 'A very pleasant evening out.'

Going down to dinner that evening, he went to the garage, and put the walking stick in the boot. It was safer there.

Hobis, the chef, excelled himself with the meal that evening, the dinner was superb. Everyone seemed to be in great spirits as the sun began to go down and most of them went out on to the terrace for after-dinner drinks.

Ellis was there with her mother but after a while they went in for coffee in the lounge.

Mary-Ann looked as glamorous as ever, while Ellis beside her wore a plain black dress and no jewellery. She did, however, smile at Tony and asked him how he had got on in London. He sat down with them.

'I went up to see a friend,' Tony said. 'We had lunch together.'

'Pity she couldn't join you down here,' Ellis said.

Her mother gave her a quick glance.

But Tony just smiled. 'Would you be free to come to look at another house tomorrow?' he said. 'I made the appointment for eleven.'

She turned to her mother, who sat glowing with pleasure, her imagination running away with her.

'You go, honey,' she said. 'I'm only popping over to the house to check something. No need for you to come with me.'

Ellis turned to Tony. 'Yes, I'd like that,' she said. 'Where is it?'

131

'Little Bristow?' he questioned. 'I think—'

'Yes, there is a village called Little Bristow. What time shall I meet you?'

'Is it far?'

'No, twenty minutes' drive from here.'

'Would half past ten be too early for you?'

'No, not at all.'

Getting up, he excused himself. 'See you tomorrow then, Ellis. Goodnight.'

'Goodnight, Tony,' they said together, and Mary-Ann sat back, as pleased as the cat that got the cream.

And so the evening passed.

Robert Markham was late coming to bed, and Grace, who was already in bed reading, kept glancing at the bedside clock wondering what was keeping him.

When he did come in eventually, he looked tired.

'What's up?' she asked, knowing that something was.

'Well, nothing, but something,' he said. 'I've just had a chat with Maggie – Maggie Dysart – the cleaning lady. She told Harris that when she did the stairs early this morning she noticed that a little picture was missing.'

'Missing? What do you mean – missing?'

'It's missing off the wall, and she's right, I've just been to look.'

She got out of bed, putting her dressing gown on.

'No need to go and look, it's gone. Although I don't think anyone would notice it. And, of course, we don't know how long it's been missing.'

'But which one was it? A large picture? How—'

'No, that's the point – it's a tiny picture, very small, but someone saw fit to reach up and take it off the wall.'

'Robert!'

'Don't like this sort of thing,' he frowned. 'I've just been into the office and looked up the inventory – it's a small picture of the artist Dudemeyer. Can't call him to mind myself, but it's a copy, not the real thing.'

'Oh, no value then. Why would anyone want to steal that?' she said. 'Not worth anything is it?'

'Shouldn't think so. My insurers will tell me but it's not worth going to the police or making a claim for.'

'What a funny thing to take. Unusual, isn't it? It didn't drop to the floor?'

'Well, dear, if it did, no one picked it up and handed it in.'

'Perhaps it was some sort of a joke?'

He disappeared into the bathroom. 'Oh, we'll get to the bottom of it, don't you worry. It might be valueless, still, it's a theft, just the same.'

Grace thought and thought but couldn't recollect it at all. 'Come and get some sleep,' she called out. 'You must be dog tired.'

Chapter Fourteen

Dot Turnbull opened the door of the charity shop on that Monday morning, Liz and Rosie behind her, tut-tutting as she saw bin bags.

'You'd think half of them couldn't read,' she said. 'Oh, well, pick 'em up, Liz and go through them. And what's this?'

There was a letter or two and a small package, which she took through to the inner room, placing them on the table.

She laughed, as she opened the packet. 'Another masterpiece,' she said. 'Price it and put it on the shelf, Rosie.'

Rosie looked at it, making a face. 'How much then?' she asked.

Dot took it from her. 'Oh, one twenty-five, though, wait a minute, the frame's quite nice, make it two twenty-five.'

'OK, Dot.'

The morning in the charity shop had begun.

It was a very quiet start to the day at Lamb Cottage. Granny Holden quietly got breakfast, not that Bernice ate much, just muesli and a piece of toast.

'Look, love, it's no good going on like this. She's here, and there is nothing we can do about it now.'

'We didn't ask her to come,' Bernice said.

'I know, but well, I have feelings too, and as her mother ...

Bernice jumped up and went over to her, putting her arms round her. 'Oh, I'm a selfish bitch, Gran. But I can't forgive her – never, I just can't.'

'I know, I know,' Granny Holden said. 'No one is expecting you to but she must have wanted to come, and that's half the battle, at least for me. I always wanted to see her again before ...'

'She, don't talk like that, you're going to live for ever,' Bernice soothed her.

'And that husband of hers is nice, she's a very lucky woman.'

'Yes, she doesn't deserve him. But he's nice, as you say.'

'Bernice, I have to tell you that today they are coming over to collect me, and taking me up to London.'

'You didn't tell me! Why didn't you tell me last night?'

'Well, you weren't in a very good mood for one thing, and another I wasn't sure if you'd like it if I went. But now I've decided to go anyway.'

Bernice glowered. 'Are you sure you feel up to it?'

'Yes, I'm excited about it.'

'You won't feel too tired?'

'Not me!' Granny Holden said. 'And they'll take care of me, I'm sure of that.'

'They'd better,' Bernice said. She picked up her handbag. 'I'd best be going or I shall be late. What time will you be back?'

'No idea,' Granny Holden said.

'Have a nice day then,' Bernice gave a weak smile.

'That's better,' Granny Holden said, giving her a kiss.

They were coming for her at ten and, as she cleared the table, and threw the crumbs out to the birds, she saw the two collar doves sitting on the cherry tree next door. They were a comfort to her, those doves, and they flew down immediately.

She locked the back door and sat down for a minute to collect her thoughts. It was such a pity, all round. But

135

Bernice had always been the same where her mother was concerned. Hated any mention of her. At first, after Carol's flight, she used to ask, 'Where's Mummy?' But after a few months, that stopped and she never mentioned her again. Once or twice early on, when Granny Holden had had post from Carol, she had tried to read the letter to her, but she wasn't having it. It was if a steel core had wrapped itself round her heart and she just didn't want to know. She grew harder too as the years went by. Went on a secretarial course, passed with honours, got herself a job which mean going into Stow, but soon gave it up after the position at The Old Manor House became vacant.

She had had one or two boyfriends, but nothing serious, it was as if there was no room for anything in her life but her Gran, Lamb Cottage and her work.

It would be nice if she could find a man friend, Granny Holden fretted. To tell the truth, when Dot Turnbull's son lost his wife, and was left with a small boy, she hoped and prayed that something might come of it with George and Bernice. But nothing ever had. Now if she was to believe Dot, he was interested in the dress-shop lady. Well, in all fairness, she was a nice woman.

As she climbed the small staircase to her room she pondered. She was a bit like her mother, Bernice. Carol had never told her who the father was – she guessed a married man, but Carol never said.

She would put it all behind her for today and enjoy her trip to London.

Sybil Collier usually woke late, unlike Kath, who was an early bird.

She sat up, wearing her hair net, and looked at the clock through narrowed eyes. Eight-thirty. No sounds from Kath next door; she had probably gone down to breakfast.

She bathed and took her rollers out, peering into the mirror to see that she had her make up on properly – her eyesight wasn't that good.

136

Dressed in a pink knitted suit and grey sweater, she looked as nice as she would ever look. She settled her glasses on her nose, made sure she had her sunglasses, picked up her handbag and made for the communicating door.

'Kath?' she called. 'Kath?' And opened the door.

She's gone down without me. Then something struck her. The bedclothes were pulled back but there was no sigh of any of Kath's clothes. Her make up had gone from the dressing table and, going over to the wardrobe, she found it empty. She had an extraordinary feeling of emptiness, of being alone and hurried down to the reception desk.

'Hello, dears,' she said, in her deep voice. 'Mrs Baxter?'

'She left a note for you, Mrs Collier,' Bernice said. 'I think she was called away, she settled her account.'

Sybil was lost for words. She sat down in the chair opposite and tore open the letter.

'Dear Sybil,' she read. 'Sorry about this but I've had enough. The eternal bickering and complaining, I'd rather be on my own. So I'm going home. I won't be there when you get there, because I am going down to visit Sarah, Kath.'

Sybil, white as a sheet, folded the letter and put it back in the envelope. She and Kath had adjacent flats, had them ever since their husbands died. Would she be back? Would she move? Kath was all right, she always made friends, but she Sybil, she relied on Kath. Too much, perhaps ...

'Thank you, dear,' she said politely and, walking tall, went into breakfast.

And then she remembered that James Elliott was going home today. He said he was here for just the week ...

Tony and Ellis were sitting having a ploughman's lunch at a nearby hotel after leaving the house at Little Bristow.

Looking up, Tony saw that Ellis was studying him covertly beneath her lashes. 'What?' he said.

'Just wondering why you waste your time going over these houses,' she said.

'I'm not wasting my time. Did you not enjoy it?'

'But you're not doing it for me, are you?' She took a piece of bread and broke it off. 'What exactly are you looking for?'

'Hard to say – none of the three I've seen is at all suitable,' he said.

'Perhaps you are looking in the wrong area.'

'Could be.'

'What a waste of time!'

'I've enjoyed it,' he said truthfully.

She took a sip of wine. 'I've told you about my love life, how has yours been?' she asked.

'What? You want all the details?'

'Well, as much as you can tell me without making me blush.' She pushed her plate away. 'On second thoughts, tell me why you want this country house? Do you fish, shoot, hunt?'

'I can fish, shoot and hunt, but I'm not a sportsman, particularly.'

'So what is your sport – women?'

He wanted to say, well, I wouldn't be with you if it was – and knew that was unkind.

'Well, I kind of amble,' he said.

'And you need a country house you can – amble in?' she said.

'I need to invest in something,' he said. 'And I get weary of London life.'

'You could start with a small cottage.'

'I would go mad in a small cottage,' he said.

'I see. So it's space you need. Rooms, and a prestigious house, not necessarily prestigious but, well "a country house",' she said.

He found himself quite believing things when he lied. After a time, they grew real. He pulled himself back to earth.

'I may give up the whole idea. I am not desperate,' he said.

'Have you ever been married?'

'You asked me that before,' he said.

'Oh sorry, and what did you say?'

'No.'

'What a scintillating conversation this is.'

'I shall know it when I see it,' he said, rising to his own defence.

'I hope I'm there when you do. I shall be intrigued. Do you have brothers, sisters?'

'One brother, one sister,' he said.

'And what do they do?'

'What's this – a cross examination?'

'OK, so, I'm nosy,' she said. 'You're a bit of a loner, aren't you? Like me?'

'Yes, you could say that.'

'And you're a financial director, something like that.'

'Yes, something like that.'

'Well, I can see you are not going to be drawn, let's go.'

'I could ask you the same sort of questions,' he began.

'Ah, but I am an open book,' Ellis said.

The two ladies – Constance and Sybil Collier – met at lunch.

'On your own today?' Constance asked politely.

She had no wish to get involved with Sybil – of the two women she preferred Kath.

'Yes, dear,' Sybil said. 'Kath was called away – nothing serious I am glad to say. But I shall stay on for a day or two, pity to waste this nice weather. London can be very unpleasant at this time of year.'

'True,' Constance agreed. Without Kath, Sybil seemed to be only half a person.

'Have you looked round the village?' Sybil asked.

'Yes, I did, the first day I came.'

'Have you been to Barbara's Pantry?' Sybil asked.

'No, I haven't.'

139

'If you are doing nothing this afternoon, why not join me for tea there?' and Sybil gave her warmest smile. 'They have the best scones and cream.'

It was on the tip of Constance's tongue to refuse but, having nothing else to do, she agreed to go.

'It's but a short walk,' Sybil said. 'I'll meet you here at three-thirty – is that all right? Give us time for a little nap,' and she gave a fairly horrific wink.

Why not? thought Constance.

She did rest, though. Going to her room, she lay down on the bed, closed her eyes – and thought about Joe.

She wished she could stop thinking about him but she supposed as she had worked in close contact with him for so long that it was difficult to get him out of her mind. Talking and exchanging views on the City with Sir John didn't help either, brought it all back.

Well, she excused herself. Forty years is a long time. And I was kingpin there. Kept everything ticking over like clockwork. At least, I think I did. Perhaps I overestimate myself. It wouldn't have been so bad if Joe hadn't proposed. Took me by surprise all right. It was like being married for forty years – almost but not quite. All physical contact had ended after five years – and whose fault was that? Both of theirs – it fizzled out – face it, she told herself. Then having the baby daughter – that just about knocked it stone dead. However, the affair had been over by then.

She got up, tired of thinking over old times. Not exactly exciting though, tea with Sybil.

She opened the wardrobe and pondered what she had with her that was suitable for her to wear. A dress would be nice . . .

A woman always wore dresses – she never saw her mother in anything else. Today, where did you find a dress? A proper dress?

The skirt and blouse she selected were nice though. Simple, yes, and old fashioned. Blow that, she wasn't young

140

any more. Afternoon tea suggested a dress, a frock . . .

Sybil was waiting for her downstairs in a well-cut trouser suit, a very elaborate heavy necklace round her neck, her hair immaculate. You had to hand it to her.

'Hello, dear,' Sybil said and, tucking her arm in Constance's walked them out of the hotel and thence to Barbara's Pantry.

It was early evening and Mary-Ann Macready was trying to decide what to wear. Something she hadn't worn before – the pale pink? She held it against herself – yes, it suited her, pink always had.

She had some pink pearls her husband had bought her on their twentieth wedding anniversary with earrings to match. Perhaps not, black jet would be nicer, too much pink would be overdone. As she picked out the jet beads, something struck her – at first she was not sure what it was. Then she realised. Something was missing – the small silk bag containing the tiepin. An easy thing to steal and she searched to make sure. Oh, Ellis would be devastated! She daren't think what she would say if she knew. The little purse was not there!

She searched the dressing-table drawers, knowing it would not be there, and felt herself flushing. Oh, she had never trusted this hotel! At all costs she must say nothing to Ellis. After a final search, she locked the jewel case and prepared to go down to see the manager, Markham, or whatever his name was.

Clutching the jewel box in its paper carrier, she approached the reception desk. 'Could I have a word with the manager? It is rather urgent.'

'I am not sure—' Bernice began.

'It is important, of the utmost importance,' Mary-Ann Macready said.

'If you would take a seat, I'll try and get hold of him,' Bernice said.

A few minutes later, Robert Markham arrived and,

greeting her, asked her to accompany him back to this office. He could see by her expression that something was wrong.

'Do sit down, Mrs Macready,' he said. 'Now, in what way can I help you?'

'Here is my jewel box – to put in the safe but I have to tell you that something is missing from it.'

He was furious at the implied suggestion but kept a cool front. Not for a moment did he believe there was any truth in it.

'A small purse is missing, containing a diamond tiepin which belonged to my husband. He left it to my daughter and I dare not tell her, she will be devastated.'

'Is is possible that your daughter—?'

'Really! Is that very likely? It is worth a great deal of money, as you may imagine.'

'I'm sure it is,' he said gently, seeing that she was indeed very upset. 'But the likelihood of it being broken into while in my care – particularly as you have the key—'

'Another key could have been used.'

'I hardly think so, and in all my time here we have never had such a thing happen before.'

'Well, there is a first time for everything,' she said grimly. 'Will you get in touch with the police, or shall I?'

'I would rather you left that to me. And I need hardly ask you to say nothing of this. I have the good name of the hotel to consider.'

'And I have my husband's memory and possessions to worry about, to say nothing of my daughter's' and she dabbed her eyes.

'I am sorry, Mrs Macready, deeply sorry that you have been put to so much worry and I will do everything in my power to unravel the mystery. I am sure there must be a logical explanation. Would you like me to send someone up to search your rooms?'

'That won't be necessary,' she said. 'It was in the jewel box, and was never used, obviously. Please see that my daughter knows nothing of this.'

'Of course, Mrs Macready,' he said and, taking her box, escorted her back to the reception desk. He made sure that the jewel box was back in the safe before he made his way back. He might have known that woman would cause trouble – hadn't she had something missing before?

Grace looked up when he came in. 'Robert? What is it? What's wrong?'

'That Macready woman,' he said.

'What's she done now?'

He slumped down in the easy chair. 'Says a valuable diamond tiepin is missing from her jewel box, suggesting someone tampered with it while in our custody.'

'You're joking! How?'

'Don't ask,' he said.

They were silent for a long time, then Grace spoke. 'Alice?' she asked.

'Definitely,' he said and picked up the phone.

Chapter Fifteen

Alice Rosemary Davis was a policewoman on extended maternity leave. She was married to a police office and they had an eighteenth-month-old daughter.

She had always wanted to go into the police force, even as a child, and later found her dream husband working alongside her. They were both passionate about their jobs and intended one day to have a private detective agency.

She was beautiful, elegant, with a happy, but probing, disposition, and she was also the middle daughter of three born to Robert and Grace Markham of The Old Manor House at Cypress Grove.

So it was with confidence that Robert telephoned her and asked for her help. It was not be the first time she had come to their rescue.

She lost no time in arriving, having left her small daughter with a friend, and duly presented herself at her parents' hotel. Robert swiftly outlined the grim tale for her and she could see the problem.

'The picture, then,' she asked. 'Do I know it?'

'I doubt you would remember it,' Robert said. 'Very small, at the top of the stairs, a copy apparently.'

'I personally wouldn't worry about that at the moment, sounds as if someone was playing games. Have you any children in the hotel?'

'No, we seldom have children staying here,' said Grace.

'Never mind, the missing tiepin is much more interesting,' she said. 'What time is dinner?'

She made a wonderful entrance just after most people were seated, a vision in a short blue dress with diamante shoulder straps. Her figure was exquisite, slim as a reed, yet filling out the right places, her hair a blonde cascade of curls, which were tied back carelessly. Ravishing blue eyes – and a warm and friendly smile.

As she passed each table she nodded a greeting and sat on her own at a corner table, while the waiter, to his pleasure, attended her.

The men all looked up from their meal, as they are wont to do when any female passed their table, and most of them did a double take when Alice walked in.

This is more like it, Tony thought. Things were looking up.

Mrs Macready sat grimly, as she had done most of the day, Ellis noticed. Something on her mind. Enviously Ellis saw the young woman partaking of her meal, the white hands, ringless, moving about the table so graciously, and looked down at her own hands. Strong, capable hands.

Sybil looked across at her, then away. Young people today, she could have done with a scarf around her shoulders.

Constance was intrigued. People always interested her. What was the young woman doing here? Holiday? Unlikely. Break from a difficult and boring job? She would have gone to Barbados or one of those sunny places you read about. She was charming, though, no doubt about that.

Ellis was fascinated. What would she be? Thirty? She was no judge of age. Less, perhaps – twenty-seven, eight? She saw Tony take a sidelong glance. Well, a man would. Stunning. She wished now she had made more effort on her own behalf. But it was her own fault. She wished she knew what was the matter with her mother. It was unusual for her to be in a mood all day.

'Mom,' she said, using the old childish term. 'Are you all right? You've been so quiet all day.'

'Yes, thanks, Ellis, I'm fine.'

'You're not worried about anything to do with the builders, are you? We could go over tomorrow.'

'No, Ellie, I'm fine.'

After dinner most of the diners made their way to the coffee lounge or the terrace. Alice went and sat outside, where the evening sun caught the gold of her hair and she moved slightly under the umbrella so the sun would not reach her face. She ordered coffee and sat back, smiling broadly at Constance, who was obliged to stop, so friendly was the greeting.

'Are you alone?' Constance asked.

The girl nodded. 'Yes, I am.'

'May I join you?' Constance said.

'Please do,' Alice said, and held out her hand. 'I'm Alice Davis.'

'Constance Boswell.'

'What a lovely evening,' the girl said.

'Beautiful,' Constance agreed.

'Have you been here long?'

'I've had a week, going into my second week, and home again on Friday,' Constance said.

'Will you be sorry to leave?' Alice asked.

'Oh, indeed I will, I have had a wonderful time – it is such a lovely hotel.'

'It is indeed,' Alice said.

'Do you know the area?' Constance said.

'Yes, very well, my family lived quite near here.'

'Oh, how nice. It was new to me, but I have been around a bit.'

'That's nice.'

Constance had an urge to know what she was doing here. Short of asking her what sort of work she did – after all, most young women did today, she was at a loss, not wishing to pry.

'Are you staying long?' she asked.

'Depends, a few days, I expect.' That seemed enough for the time being, and they sat drinking their coffee.

Then Constance took the plunge. 'I have just retired from the City – London, I mean. I worked in an office, PA to the director – and taking my first holiday since I left.'

'Oh, how wonderful,' Alice said, and looked as if she meant it. 'So you're a Londoner?'

'Well, I was born in Essex, but I've lived most of my life in London.'

'I live in London too,' Alice said. 'Putney.'

'Oh, nice area,' Constance said. 'Do you work?'

'Oh yes, I'm taking a few days off. I've been so busy this last few weeks, I thought I deserved it.'

'I know the feeling,' Constance smiled.

'I work in a government office,' the girl said. 'Whitehall, and sometimes the pressure is very great.'

'Oh,' Constance said feelingly. 'I can imagine.' Somehow she knew she had an important job.

'I come here because I know the area and it is so peaceful and quiet.'

Constance thought how lovely she was. How awful to be trapped in a government office. Yet she had been trapped – all those years in the City. She wanted to say to her – get out now, while you are still young. She was the daughter she would have like to have had.

The cottage seemed empty without Gran. Bernice thought she would rather be out of the way when they got back but it was too early to go to bed.

She had lunched at the hotel – that was always a bonus – good food prepared for you. Now she made a cup of tea and sat thinking, before deciding to go for a walk.

It was a lovely evening – June had been wonderful this year – so nice for all the visitors – and she wandered out of the cottage, up the High Street, looking in all the windows. Genella's window looked very enticing but she herself was not into smart clothes. As long as she was well dressed for the hotel, there was no point in dressing up.

She walked on until she came to the green. There were a few people about, some on the seats, the cypress trees in the background, children playing with a ball, it was so nice to relax. It was a long time since she had been up here. She sat back and closed her eyes.

She would try not to think of the situation she found herself in. Hard to know what might happen. But Gran was safe with her and in a few days that woman – the woman who called herself Mother – would be flying back to the States. Good riddance.

A shadow fell across her eyes and she opened them to see a small boy regarding her.

'Excuse me, could I get my ball? It's under your seat.'

'Of course,' she said. What a nice little boy – polite too. Then the tall figure of a man loomed up beside him.

He stopped short, and smiled. 'Bernice, isn't it? Bernice Holden?'

'Good Lord! George Turnbull!'

They had attended the village school together. How long was it since she had seen him?

The small boy still stood waiting.

'Oh, sorry, of course you can,' she said as she stood up. 'Thank you.' Locating his ball, he ran off . . .

'Well, this a surprise,' George said, sitting down beside her. 'How long is it since we met?'

'Don't ask! Donkey's years,' Bernice said, but she was pleased to see him.

He had moved to London after his marriage and she knew of course that his wife had died. Dot, his mother, was Gran's friend. She had heard that he moved back to the Cotswolds but thought no more of that.

'Are you visiting your mother?' she asked, looking at

him. Gosh – what a handsome man he was! He didn't look like that when they were at school. Once they left, their paths had divided, his to London, and hers to a secretarial course locally.

'No, I'm living here now,' he said. 'Well, nearby, at Akers Green. We've been there four months.'

'That's a nice little village.'

He took a sidelong glance at her. His mother had mentioned her problem to him with the visiting Americans and he thought it couldn't be easy. She was still pretty, but not overly so, with auburn hair, rather nice green eyes, and a set to her mouth which looked permanent. Slightly grim, for a young woman. They were about the same age ...

'How is your gran?' he asked. 'Mum told me she'd been to see her.' Better not ask about the visiting daughter.

'She's fine, getting on, you know, but she's fit as a fiddle.'

They were interrupted by a breathless little boy.

'My son Mark,' George said. 'What's up?'

'Those boys have taken my ball.'

'Have you asked for it back?'

'Yes, but they won't give it back.'

'Oh, well, a bit of diplomacy then – excuse me, Bernice.'

She watched him as he walked across the green. He had grown into a very nice man. All those years since she had seen him ...

A few minutes later, he returned holding Mark's hand who clutched the ball in his other hand.

'This is Bernice – Bernice Holden – Granny Holden's granddaughter,' George explained.

He put a hand out, had obviously been taught to do so. 'I'm Mark,' he said, 'Mark Turnbull.' And ran off.

'How old is he?'

'Six, last week.'

'He's great,' she said, looking after him.

'Well, Bernice, tell me about you.'

'What's to tell?' she answered. 'I work at The Old Manor House, have done for years, as I expect your mother told you. A fixture, you could say.'

A chip on her shoulder, definitely, he thought. What a pity. She obviously had a problem and knew it was to do with her mother, who had left her. Having a wonderful mother himself, it was difficult to imagine.

'You must come over and see the cottage, when and if you have time,' he said. 'White cottage, in the High Street, in Akers Green.'

'I'd like that,' she said, turning to look at him straight in the eyes. Lovely green eyes, but a bit sad, he thought.

They talked for another fifteen minutes until Mark said he wanted to go home now.

'Say goodnight to Bernice,' George said.

'I'll be in touch,' he said to Bernice, who stayed on the seat, waiting for the sun to go down.

It was not until lunch the next day that Alice got a chance to speak to the Macreadys.

Visitors came and went – the newly marrieds had left at the weekend and the Americans had arrived. James Elliott had gone, as had Kath Baxter, but Sir John was still there. A new elderly couple arrived, who were very reserved and seemed not to want to talk to anyone.

After lunch the next day it started to rain slightly, enough to prevent people having coffee outside. As Alice left the dining room and went into the coffee lounge, Mary-Ann Macready smiled warmly at her and patted the chair beside her.

'Do join us,' she said.

'Thank you,' Alice said graciously and took the seat beside them.

'I'm Mary-Ann Macready, and this is my daughter, Ellis.'

'How do you do – Alice Davis,' she said, with a ravishing smile.

Ellis thought she looked even better close up than at a distance.

'This is nice,' Alice said brightly. 'I am looking forward to my few days' holiday.'

'Just a few days?'

'Yes, just two or three, it depends.'

'You have to get back to – work?' Mary-Ann asked, wanting to know what she did.

'Yes. I'm afraid so,' Alice said. 'However, even a few days is a change.'

'And what are you doing in this part of the world?' she asked. 'You are American, aren't you?'

'Yes,' Mary-Ann said. 'And proud of it. I married an Englishman and came to live over here.'

'Where exactly?' Alice asked.

'Not far from here – Charter Hall – but I am having the house done over and needed to get out of the way and this seemed a perfect solution.'

'Perfect, I would say,' Alice agreed.

At that moment, Tony brushed passed them, excusing himself, and went towards the lift.

'My word, what a handsome man!' Alice said, and noticed that Ellis blushed furiously.

So, that's the way of it, she thought.

'Yes,' Mary-Ann said, ever pleased to be able to know someone worthwhile. 'Tony Sheridan – he is staying here, I understand he is looking for a house in the area.'

'Oh, very nice too,' Alice said. 'There are quite a few lovely houses roundabout.'

'Yes, Ellis went with him to see one, didn't you, darling?'

Ellis looked daggers. 'Just to accompany him, he thought a woman's point of view might be useful,' she said, dragging out the words.

'Well, yes – I agree with that,' Alice said. 'And was it nice?'

'I thought so but he didn't seem to be impressed,' Ellie said.

So, she has been out with him, Alice thought. Mustn't arouse suspicion at this stage. 'Excuse me, I must be going, I am expecting a telephone call from my fiancé.'

'Oh, you are engaged?'

Alice smiled.

'Oh, that's lovely. You must be a very happy young woman.'

Alice dimpled. 'Oh, I am. Goodnight then, Mary-Ann, Ellis.'

'What a nice young woman.'

She gave a swift glance at Ellis's face. She was frowning and no one looked more forbidding than Ellis when she was frowning.

'Ellie, dear, do take that look off your face. You look so cross. Why don't we go out to Cirencester tomorrow, or Cheltenham, and find you some lovely things to wear?'

'Oh, Mother!' Ellis said. As if that was the answer to her problem . . .

Alice reported what little she had to say to her parents later that night.

'So our little American has been out with Tony Sheridan at least once,' she said. 'He is looking for a house, a country house.'

Robert frowned. 'Yes, I know, he told me that.'

'Also, I've done some checking. Interesting. By the way, he has no "form" as we say but once was thought to have been a lookout man for a jewellery gang – nothing proved.'

'What!' Robert was shocked.

'And by the way, what address did I see in the register?'

'Cadogan Square,' Robert said.

Alice shook her head. 'Not so,' she said. 'Number 14, Timble Street, Notting Hill.'

'No!' Grace said.

'But,' and she knew they were hanging on her words, 'You did know he was the younger son of Lord Redingham?'

She picked up her handbag. 'You can close your mouths now, I'm off to bed. Night, sleep well.' And she kissed them both.

Chapter Sixteen

Bernice sat on the seat for a long time after George and Mark had gone. Sat while the sun slowly sank in the west, going over and over past events and trying to make sense of it all.

There was no point in going back to the cottage yet. They would not return until late, particularly if they had been to a theatre; Gran would have loved that. She had offered several times to take her to London, but Gran always refused. 'Too much effort, dear, I'm getting past trips to London.' But this time she had gone – with two stalwarts like Carol and her husband.

Well, it was nice for her. She could understand that. What she couldn't understand was how people expected her to forgive Carol for what she had done. Thinking again about it, although she usually managed to put it to the back of her mind, she still could not understand how a mother could leave a little girl – just five years old – and clear off to the States, and not return until now . . .

She would never forgive her. Had hardened her heart to such an extent that she was no longer interested. It was nice for Gran, Carol was her daughter, and presumably she had forgiven her. But not Bernice. It was as if her heart was made of stone where her mother was concerned. It took a cold and unforgiving nature to do a thing like that.

As she sat, she thought of her beloved Gran. She

wouldn't go on for ever – and she had always put off thinking about that time. At the moment, she had a good job, was content enough, the days ticked by. She supposed most people would find it boring. She would have liked to have children, but it was unlikely now. She had never been one for lots of boyfriends, it was a pity, but she supposed a lot of it was due to her background: the knowledge that she had not been wanted; her mother didn't care about her and she built a carapace around herself so she would not get hurt again.

She glanced at her watch and saw that it was nine-thirty, and the sun had almost gone down. Time to make a move.

A breeze had sprung up; she walked across the green, remembering how Gran used to take her there with other children. A doll's pram, and hoops and skipping ropes – such fun they had had. Spring evenings, after school in frosty and snowy weather, they had even tried toboggans at one stage but the snow was never really deep enough for that.

It was nice to see George again. He had had a tragic life – or a tragic married life. For his wife to die so young, leaving that nice little boy. When he moved to London she had quite lost touch with him, except that Gran kept up a close friendship with his mother, Dot Turnbull. When he left Cypress Grove for London, he married a London girl, and lived up there. Now he was back. She would like to see him again – they had something in common – their childhood.

When she got home, she was surprised to find Gran in her dressing gown getting ready for bed.

'Oh, Gran!' She kissed her warmly. 'I didn't think you'd be back yet.'

'Yes, we got back about nine,' Gran said. 'It was lovely.'

'Where did you go?'

'We went to a matinée and afterwards Dwight took us out to dinner in the Strand. It brought back old times, I can tell you.'

And the old eyes sparkled. 'Carol said she'd get back. We didn't know where you'd gone. She wished you goodnight.'

'I'm sorry I missed her,' lied Bernice. 'Now, you get upstairs to bed. Would you like anything else?'

'No, thank you, after that meal, I just want to sleep.'

'Goodnight then, Gran.'

'Goodnight, dear.'

What had she done with herself, Gran wondered, taking the stairs slowly as Bernice locked up.

After showering and shaving, Tony Sheridan sat contemplating the brochure he had received that morning. Glancing through it, he had to admit it sounded wonderful.

But what was he doing – messing about like this? Reflecting – the little picture, he should have kept it as a keepsake, perhaps not – but the tiepin? He really hated the thought of returning that. It was now as clear as a bell to him that he was never going to get near the Macready jewels, so he might as well give up right now. Somehow, Ellis's face kept appearing before him. She was such a mixed-up kid. He had never met anyone like her before: such honesty, not usually met with in his world, plain speaking, no beating about the bush.

He would leave on Friday, no point in staying over, but he would go to see one last house, this one to justify his stay at The Old Manor House and he would ask Ellis to go with him. He enjoyed her company, although you never knew what she was going to say next.

And he wouldn't mind seeing a bit more of that young beauty, Alice. The day was young and he must plan a campaign.

He put through a call to Ellis.

'Good morning,' he said.

'Hi,' Ellis said.

'Feel like going over another house?' he asked. This one sounds more like the sort of thing I want – and we could

156

go today – or tomorrow. Just as you like.'

Unknown to him Ellie's eyes were shining. Of course she would like it – but why did he keep asking her?

'What time are you thinking of going?' she asked.

'Any time, before lunch, or this afternoon. Which would suit you?'

'I have some things to do for Ma, telephone calls, queries, could we make it after lunch?'

'Sure, I'll give the agents a ring. See you in the bar at two-thirty.'

Having arranged to be at the house at three-thirty, he went downstairs into the bar after lunch, but most people were outside.

Once Ellis had arrived, they went on to the terrace where Alice was sitting, clad in the briefest sundress, which showed off her beautiful figure. She wore a large sun hat, which flattered her as well as keeping the sun off her face.

After they had greeted each other, Alice suggested they join her.

Gosh, but she was lovely, thought Ellis. Her dress so brief, gloriously suntanned; Ellis was so envious she could have wept. She had to admit Alice was a nice young woman ... wonderful teeth, great smile.

'Well,' Alice said, 'and what have you been up to?'

'Not a lot,' Ellis said. She was wearing white culottes and a black top. A scarf was tied around her head, and she wore dark glasses.

'How is your mother, well?'

'Yes, she's fine but so busy to and froing with the workmen and telephone calls. I'm pleased she is here away from it all.'

'It's Charter Hall isn't it?' Alice asked. Ellis smiled.

'Yes, Charter Hall, not far from Oxford.'

'I think I've seen it on my travels, Georgian, isn't it?'

'Yes, it belonged to my father, a family house.'

'And that's what you hope to find, isn't it, Tony?' She looked at him under her lashes.

157

He nodded, 'Yes, with a bit of luck.'

'Tell me what you've seen, I know the area quite well.'

'A house on Dell Bank Common, a rather grand house,' Ellie said. 'I think that was the nicest,' she added.

'But not suitable for you?' Alice asked Tony kindly.

Tony shook his head. 'No, I'm not sure what it was but definitely not for me.'

'What was the other one?' Ellis asked. 'The one we saw on your birthday?'

'The day before,' Tony interjected. 'When we went to lunch.'

'That's right.'

'Lucknow Grange,' he said.

So, they had become quite friendly. And his birthday – how did Ellis know that? Hadn't they just met?

Alice sighed deeply. 'And no luck yet?' she said. 'Well, something will turn up.'

'I hope so, for I leave on Friday.' And Alice saw Ellis throw him a quick glance. She didn't know ...

'I have to get back – lots to do. Still, I'll be back. Ah, here's the waiter. What will you have?'

Alice sat back thinking – they were quite friendly. Had they known each other before? And he had had a birthday. It was clear to everyone that Ellis liked him – more than somewhat. Had she perhaps given him a birthday gift? Of jewellery? Of a solitaire diamond pin?

She was sure of it. There was no way anyone could have got to those jewels once they were in the safe.

'You must come and have a drink with me this evening and let me know how you got on,' she said.

'That would be nice,' Ellis said.

'When would you have to get back?' Tony asked Alice.

'Oh, to London you mean, by weekend. Before if I can make it, it's just been a short break.'

Tony wondered what she did – it sounded important. He looked at her with admiring eyes, which Ellis was quick to notice. Ah, the luck of the draw. Anyway, he's

158

not my type. Not down to earth enough, lives up there in his aristocratic English world. Not like Johnnie, she reflected, then realised that she hadn't thought of him for quite some time ...

Driving along the country lanes, Ellis beside him, Tony realised it really had been a break. A change from his old haunts – a bit of a waste of time – but he had enjoyed it. He fell to wondering about Alice – she really was stunning – more his type, but she was so much like the girls he met in London, there was no novelty about her.

Here was this strange girl, sitting beside him, the oddest girl he had ever been out with – if you could call it that. He would be bored stiff going on his own and he had to keep up appearances. Even that nice girl, Bernice, at the reception desk had wished him a nice day and hoped that he had some luck finding what he wanted.

'Where exactly is it?' he asked Ellis.

'Take the road to Cheltenham – about a mile further on – and I'll give you directions from there.'

She looked through the brochure. 'It looks lovely, Tony. Historic Grade II listed house. Family house, sitting deep in the countryside, and with planning permission – that's a bonus, reception hall, three reception rooms, six bedrooms, four bathrooms, stabling, stone outbuildings, paddocks. Do you really want a house as large as that?'

'I want a family at some stage of my life.'

He wasn't as tough as he thought was was, she mused. Of course he wanted a family, every real man did ... and she imagined living in such a house as his wife – then smiled.

'What are you smiling at?'

'Nothing,' she said. 'Just so pleasant to be here.'

This time it was a woman from the agent's who showed them over and it turned out to be all the blurb had said.

Sitting in lush countryside, it nevertheless was a commanding house – a house you certainly could be proud of. Elegant rooms, empty now, since the owners had left, but a housekeeper in residence in the lodge at the entrance gate.

Surely, Ellis thought, he can't find fault with this one.

He followed them up the stairs and into the rooms, hands behind his back – until you would have thought it was Ellis buying the house. Several times, she frowned at him as though to bring him to life and by the time the visit was over, which had taken half an hour, she had lost all patience with him.

She smiled at the agent sweetly. 'Have you had any offers yet?'

'Yes, quite a few, but none at the asking price. So you would be free to—'

'Quite,' Tony interrupted. 'I think that is all for the time being.' He gave her one of his nicest smiles, took Ellis's arm and propelled her towards the door.

'Thank you so much,' he smiled. 'Quite a lot to think about. Come Ellis.'

She got in the car and sat beside him silently.

'Shall we stop on the way back for some tea?' he asked.

'No, thank you. Not for me.'

He was disappointed but drove on, waiting for the tirade to start. A mile or so farther on, he stopped the car and turned to face her. 'Look, Ellie—'

But she was silent. Her look was enough.

'It can take years to find the right house,' he said lamely.

'I'm sure, but why do I get the impression you are not concentrating enough on what you do see?'

'What do you mean?'

'Well, you don't ask the obvious questions.'

'Like what?'

'Where is the boiler room? The central heating?'

'It's all in the blurb—'

'Oh, come on, even I am more interested than you are.'

'You're a woman, you get down to facts, I observe, take note.'

160

'Oh, is that what you do?'

This was a pointless conversation, he decided. And after all, he did not have to explain his presence in Cypress Grove to anyone. A businessman taking a holiday – that's all it need have been.

He started up the car and Ellis was left with a feeling of disappointment that it had ended like this. She had so enjoyed these outings. Still, if he was going home on Friday she would never see him again. But she knew in her heart that she was going to miss him.

Tony went down early for a pre-dinner drink but there was no sign of Ellis and so he dined alone. Alice had looked forward to hearing about the latest house but she was disappointed.

Had they quarrelled, she wondered.

She had a brief chat with Constance Boswell and Sir John, who was an interesting man, and he and Constance seemed to be getting on like a house on fire.

The two Americans were absent, perhaps visiting their daughter who lived in the village.

When she got up to leave, there was no sign of Tony Sheridan – he had either gone for a walk or gone to bed.

It was time for her to make her report to her parents. She looked forward to that.

Alice hugged her parents, she was fond of both of them, and they had waited eagerly for anything she might have discovered.

'Well, poppets,' she said. 'I am afraid I have drawn a blank.'

They sat in the comfortable flat, each with a bedtime drink.

'Indeed,' Robert said, with a gleam in his eye. 'We have had more luck, if you can call it that.'

She was alert in an instant.

He went over to the sideboard and brought out a small

161

packet and handed it to her. 'Our picture,' he said.

'The missing picture?' she asked as she unwrapped it. 'Good Lord! Is this it? Hardly a Rembrandt, is it? Where did you get it?'

'Maggie Dysart, one of the cleaners, saw it in the charity shop window, went in and bought it.'

'You're joking!'

'No, I'm not. It was priced at two pounds and twenty-five pence. She went in and bought it, I paid her, and, well, much ado about nothing.'

'Somebody is playing games ... Of course, nothing serious. Can I borrow this for a day or two?'

'Yes, of course, but you surely don't think?'

'I'm not sure what I think, yet,' Alice said. 'No news of the missing tiepin?'

He shook his head.

'You know what I think about that – I am almost sure that Ellis Macready gave it to his lordship for his birthday.'

Grace shook her head. 'I can't go along with that, they hardly know each other.'

'Well, we'll see, but Mrs Macready has not contacted you again?'

'No, she was happy, she said, to leave it in my hands, with the aid of the police.'

'Very wise,' Alice said.

Tomorrow morning, she decided, she must make a swift trip to town.

Bertrand Meyer was a friend of long standing. Alice had first met him during her investigation of certain art thefts and she knew he was an expert on Dudemeyer.

She did not expect to find anything out particularly at this stage but any help he could give her might be useful.

She arrived just after lunch at his premises in Poland Street and he greeted her warmly.

'It's very nice of you to give me your time, Bertrand,' she said. And he thought, as he always did, that marriage

162

and motherhood had not changed her. She was still as astute and as beautiful as ever.

Alice dived into her handbag and brought out a small packet.

'Just a simple query – have you see this before – and what is it?'

He looked at her, then again at the picture, his loyalty stretched in two directions.

'Sit down, my dear,' he said, peering at it closely through his magnifying glass.

'Well it is not an original but it is a self portrait of Dudemeyer. Someone – quite good – has copied it. I don't know if it's a one-off or if they churn these things out at galleries but I wouldn't have thought he was popular enough to warrant that.'

'You haven't answered my question,' she smiled.

'Oh, you mean have I seen it before? No, I can't say that I have,' he said. Now what was young Sheridan up to . . . 'Certainly not this one, although I have seen the original life size, of course.'

'Not worth a bean, is it?'

'No, my dear. Not a cent – will you stay for coffee?'

'No, Bertrand, I have to get back. I just had to make sure,' she smiled.

'Any – problem?' he asked.

'No, but thanks for your help.'

'Any time, my dear,' he said, showing her the door. 'Take care.'

Sensitive to people's reactions, she had noticed at once that Bernard had seen the little picture before but knew, being as valueless as it was, someone had been playing games. Someone like Tony Sheridan. Pity they had nothing definite on him – otherwise there might have been finger-prints.

She had enjoyed her few days at The Old Manor House and it was always great to see her parents. Personally, she thought the small picture was much ado about nothing, but the tiepin, that was different and, unless she was totally wrong, it had been given as a gift to Tony Sheridan from Ellis Macready.

It had crossed her mind that Sheridan was going over these houses with a view to possible housebreaking and indeed that might be the case but somehow she didn't think so.

She would tell her parents that they must tackle Mrs Macready and suggest that her daughter had made an *ex gratia* gift to Tony Sheridan. That way, it might all be sorted out.

But they were not going to believe her, of course . . .

Chapter Seventeen

The telephone rang in Genella Hastings's dress shop just as she was checking the day's takings preparatory to closing and she was curious to hear who might be phoning her at this hour.

'Genella Hastings.'

'Oh, Gen,' ex-husband Alan's favourite name for her.

'Alan, hello.'

'Genella, I need to see you.' His voice sounded urgent.

'What is it? What's wrong?' One of the children? His wife?

'May I come round – you're not doing anything?'

'No, of course you may. You sound worried – can't you tell me over the phone?'

Funny how her heart always raced when she heard his voice, after all this time ... Water under the bridge now ...

'No, Genella, I can't. I have to see you.'

'Well, come round then. I'll expect you, say – six-thirty.'

It would take him three-quarters of an hour to drive from Oxford.

She locked the door of the salon safely behind her and took Charlie's lead off the peg. She put out his food and water and opened the windows wide. Ah, that was better after such a warm day. She could do with air conditioning, but it was expensive. But the business only just ticked over, although it was the only dress shop in Cypress Grove. So many people today shopped in the larger towns or by catalogue. Only the one-offs came to her establishment but she was grateful for them.

She couldn't imagine why Alan wanted to see her so urgently and, truth to tell, rather than prepare a hurried meal, would have liked to have dined out. So seldom did she get the chance. But she would see. She could always rustle something up if needed.

She cleaned her face, it was remarkable how grimy it was after a day in the shop, brushed her hair and put on some lightweight trousers and a top. Into some comfy slippers – ah, bliss – and poured herself a glass of wine.

When the doorbell rang, Charlie leapt out of his basket and began to bark. She pointed to his basket. 'To bed, Charlie. To bed.' He looked up at her reproachfully as she pressed the button to allow Alan in and saw that he was pale under his tan, his eyes strained, his mouth set in a grim line.

'Sit down, Alan, you look awful.'

'I feel awful,' he said collapsing into a chair. 'Could I?' pointing to her glass of wine.

'Of course – red?' She knew that was his preference and poured him a large glass, then sat down opposite him.

'Is it one of the children?' she knew how he adored them.

He wasted no time. 'Myra has left me,' he said.

She felt stunned by the shock. 'Left you?' she repeated. 'What on earth do you mean? What about the children?'

'The children – oh, yes, she's taken them – but that won't be for long. She won't get away with that, I can tell you.'

'You'd better begin at the beginning,' she said.

'I didn't tell you when I saw you before but she is pregnant.'

Genella's eyes opened wide. 'Oh! then why?'

166

'Not mine,' he said, and this really was a shock. She had imagined they were very happily married. He had never said anything about his wife to her, she just imagined that they were happy, although it did cross her mind now and again that it was unusual for an ex-husband to visit his ex-wife quite so often as Alan came to visit her.

'What happened?'

'She's nearly four months' pregnant and I naturally assumed it was mine. It wasn't until last night when we had a bit of an argument, that it came out. She has been seeing this man for almost a year and I had no idea.'

'But how did she manage that?'

'At odd hours, she says. 'In the day time usually. The children, you know, are at school and if she can't collect them, a friend does. Anyway, she says she's seen this bloke during the daytime so naturally I never suspected. Not a clue.'

'What made her tell you, eventually?'

'I think she had just had enough and had to spill the beans.'

'Were you as shocked – as I am?'

'Yes, you can imagine. I didn't think we were blissfully happy but we ticked over, like most other married couples, we both worked, life was a bit hectic.'

'Forgive my asking – but the two little girls – are yours?'

'Oh, yes, no doubt of that – they even look like me.' He looked awful, Genella thought. What a shock.

'She's not so young, either, is she?' she asked gently.

'No, forty-two. A bit older than I am. And I have to say, we hadn't been – that close – for some time but I just assumed – her age – you know.'

'No, don't tell me any of the details,' Genella said. 'And you are absolutely sure this child is another man's child?'

'Oh, no doubt of it. She was proud of it. And then she said she was leaving.'

Genella waited.

'There was a long argument. We didn't get to bed until

167

two this morning but she was adamant. She couldn't go on any longer in a loveless marriage, as she called it.'

Genella looked at him. 'You do love her?'

'She's the mother of my children,' he said.

'That's not answering my question.'

How could he tell her? Not with the binding love I had for you – have for you – always will have ...

'Of course, like any other married couple, after ten years ...'

'Yes,' she said slowly, 'it's not a lifetime. What are you going to do?'

He stared out of the window. 'What can I do? She's left me, taking the children with her. I got home early from the office and she'd gone.' He looked at breaking point.

'Perhaps she will be back.'

'Not if I know her,' he said.

'Oh, poor man – she wanted to put her arms around him. After all, they too had been married almost ten years – well, nine to be exact. She had given him his freedom so that he might marry again and have the children he so desperately wanted and that she couldn't give him.

'Anyway,' he said. 'I didn't get to sleep at all last night and I decided I shall fight her for the children, Gen. There is no way she is going to get away with that.'

'But won't they say the mother is best for the children?'

'Oh, sod that,' he said. 'Now she is having another man's child, she can live with that. Those kids are mine. I don't mind sharing them but I'll fight to see she doesn't get sole custody.'

'Yes, I can understand that,' Genella said.

He sat staring into space.

'You don't know where she has gone?'

'No idea, to this other chap's house, I suppose.'

'And you don't think she'll come back, when she's thought it over?'

'Not her!' he said. 'Once her mind is made up.' He looked grim and then buried his face in his hands. 'But it's the girls, Gen. My little girls – I don't even know where they are.'

She put an arm round his shoulders. 'Tell you what, finish your drink and I'll run the shower and you can freshen up. And why don't we go out for a meal?'

He looked shocked.

'I could knock up something here but it's more cheerful to go out and you need cheering up.'

'Come on,' she pleaded. 'You know where the bathroom is. Let me get you some towels.'

It might have been like old times. She sat still, long after he had gone to shower. Who would have thought this would happen? Myra seemed a nice enough woman but with desires like anyone else, she supposed. But taking the children – that was hard. Surely she didn't think she would get away with that?

'OK?' she called through the door.

'OK' he called back.

How odd to have a man in my bathroom after all this time, Genella thought. Life was full of surprises. She went to telephone The Old Manor House.

She knew it was Bernice who answered, knew her voice. 'Bernice, it's Genella.'

To say Bernice was surprised was to say the least of it.

'Bernice, do you happen to have a spare table for two this evening' and she glanced at her watch, 'in about fifteen minutes?'

'Yes, we can manage that,' Bernice said.

'Oh, good,' Genella said. 'See you then. In my name. OK?'

When Alan returned from the bathroom he looked a little better, fresher, not so drained and slightly more relaxed.

'I've booked dinner at The Old Manor House,' she said, as he expostulated. 'My treat, I insist, you need cheering up.'

They were there in no time and entering the flower laden-vestibule, Robert was on hand to greet them and they were led to the table near the window.

'This is a treat,' Alan said.

'I thought you needed one.'

He looked across the table at her.

How could he tell her that the quarrel was about her – as it was on so many occasions. Myra's insistence that he had never got over her, that he still loved her, despite being married to someone else. He tried to reassure her, always had, bit it was difficult to hide the truth. He had never felt about any woman as he had about Genella and the fact that she had left him so he could marry someone to give him the family he so wanted had only served to cement his love for her. You could assume that Myra was noble enough to give up her marriage but to be seeing another man – that he could never forgive . . .

In reception, Bernice sat pensively staring at nothing. Wasn't the man with Genella her ex-husband? She knew he visited her occasionally but never on dates, as it were. She couldn't help wondering . . . After all, the last thing she had heard was that George Turnbull had asked her to little Mark's party.

The telephone rang and she answered with such a wonderful smile that Phyllida stared at her.

'Who is it?'

But Bernice shook her head.

Later on that evening Bernice returned home to find Carol and Dwight with her grandmother. They had been out somewhere for the day, which was natural enough for this was Dwight's first visit to England and he wanted to see as much as possible of the English countryside.

'Did you have a nice day?' she asked politely, ignoring Carol who still wore the nervous expression she had when she arrived. But there was no way that Bernice was going to let her off the hook.

Dwight, though, seemed impervious to any undercurrents

that there might be, and, manlike, launched into details of their visit to most of the Cotswold villages which he thought delightful.

'We have nothing at home like them,' he said.

'Yes, it is pretty countryside,' Bernice said pleasantly, 'but like everywhere else, when you get used to it you take it for granted.'

'And how is Gran today?' she asked, sending her a warm, loving look. No doubt where her affections lie, thought Carol.

'Oh, it was lovely,' Gran said. 'I'd forgotten how pretty some of those little places are although I grew up with them, as you might say. 'Course, some of them have altered, grown bigger.'

'Everywhere has changed,' Carol said shortly.

'We had dinner in a dear little pub in Burford,' Dwight said, 'old flagstones on the floor, narrow little passages – it was as much as I could do to get through them the ceilings were so low.'

'Makes you think people must have been much smaller in the old days,' smiled Bernice. She couldn't have been more pleasant, Gran was pleased to notice. Had she but known it, Bernice was making a huge effort to keep the final days peaceful. She couldn't wait for her mother to go.

'Well, I'm for bed,' she said, picking up her handbag, and going over to Gran.

'Just a minute, dear' Gran said. 'As you know, Carol and Dwight are going back to the States on Sunday and they thought we should have some kind of celebration. A dinner party – over at the hotel.'

Her look at Bernice said, 'Don't disappoint me, please, Bernice.'

'Oh.'

'Do you think they will have a table free on Saturday evening?' Gran asked.

'It's a bit late for booking but for how many?'

'Well,' Carol put in. 'There would be Dwight, and Gran, and you and I'd like Dot Turnbull to come, she's always been so good to Gran and to make up the numbers, perhaps her son, George. A real party. How old is George's son?'

'He's six,' Gran said.

'Look, this is to be a farewell party, a celebration for me, seeing my daughter again after all these years,' said Carol. Bernice turned away.

'Anyway,' Carol continued brightly, 'how about that? A dinner party, for seven. Do they take children at the hotel?'

'Of course,' Bernice said swiftly, 'but he's a bit young to be out late.'

'Well, then, a luncheon party. Would you prefer that, Mum?'

'Saturday lunch,' Gran said. 'Perhaps that's a good idea. I don't like late nights myself.'

'That's settled that, then. Saturday lunch for seven. I'd love to see young George again. I remember him as a little boy and now he has a youngster of his own and life hasn't been all kind to him. I was really shocked when Mum wrote and told me.'

How about life for me, Bernice thought acidly. She would never forgive her, never.

'We'll make it a real celebration. I hope they can come. I'll give Auntie Dot a ring in the morning, perhaps she'll ask George. Of course, if he's busy ...'

Oh, I do hope he isn't, Bernice wished silently. I would really look forward to seeing him again.

'Well,' she said aloud, 'I'll book a table for seven, shall I? Then if they can't come, at least there will be four of us.'

But to herself, just get this woman out of my life and let things get back to normal.

'Thank you, dear,' Carol said.

I expect she means well, Bernice thought – but she is not getting round me. Gran gave her a special hug when she kissed her goodnight.

172

I am a bitch, Bernice muttered, but I can't change now.

Constance Boswell had missed Sir John. He had had an important meeting in the City to attend, one of four in the year, he explained, and was not sure that he would be back for dinner.

She sighed as she picked up her handbag and made for the lift. Tomorrow she would be on her way home but she was determined not to leave until after lunch. Make the most of every minute, that was her motto now. It had been a lovely stay and, on reflection had gone so quickly. She might just have time to go into the village in the morning – she was determined to buy something as a memento in that lovely shop.

In the meantime, an after-dinner cup of coffee, still time to get out on to the terrace before the sun went down. Such an evening, with the sun sinking low over the fields. It was still warm – how she would miss it. Yet London was her home and it would be good to get back to it. She hadn't relaxed as easily as she had hoped as Joe had taken up a lot of her thoughts, which was perfectly natural when you thought about it.

She was about to leave and go up to bed, when Sir John came hurrying through the terrace doors and greeted her.

'Hello, my dear, I was hoping I would find you still up. It's a splendid evening, isn't it?'

The waiter was at his side immediately.

'A brandy, please, and will you join me, Constance?'

'No, I won't thank you but you go ahead.'

The waiter disappeared and Sir John relaxed. 'Oh,' he sighed. 'Lots of traffic, I suppose being Friday night. I can't complain – I didn't leave the City until late and met some old friends.'

'So you enjoyed your day?' she smiled.

'Yes, I did. And what sort of day did you have, my dear?'

'A restful sort of day,' she said.

When the waiter brought his brandy, he toasted her. 'Here's to a safe journey back. I hope we meet again some-time. What time are you leaving tomorrow?'

'Not until after lunch. I intend to do some last-minute shopping,' she explained.

'Ah.' He put his glass down on the table. 'By the way, I met your old boss at the meeting.'

Her heart lurched uncomfortably. 'Joe?'

'Yes, he was at the meeting at the Guildhall. We had a nice long chat.'

'You didn't – did you tell him that you had met me – here?'

'Well, I did. I hope you don't mind. You know, my dear, he misses you.'

And the telltale blush came again. How ridiculous in a woman of her age. 'Well, I daresay,' she said firmly, 'After forty years ...'

He took a sidelong glance at her. 'May I be frank?'

'Of course, John,' she said.

'You know, you didn't tell me that he had proposed marriage to you. It was a blow to him when you refused to consider marrying him.'

'Oh! He didn't tell you?' She was shocked. Two elderly gentlemen taking like two schoolgirls ...

'Yes, he did. We are old friends. Seemed quite cut up. Of course, it doesn't help that the new woman, his new PA, can't hold a candle to you.'

And she was pleased, of course, she was. No one likes to think they have been superceded by someone better, more efficient.

Of course, if Joe was in any kind of trouble, she would help him, of course she would. Forty years in the paper trade must count for something.

'Well, I must get going. I may see you at breakfast.'

'Yes, I hope so.'

'If not, I hope you have a wonderful visit to your daughter.'

174

'I'm sure I shall.' His eyes twinkled back at her.
'Goodnight, John, Sleep well.'
'You too, Constance.'

Chapter Eighteen

It was a late night for Grace and Robert Markham – a busy weekend brewing up and the usual change of residents.

'It's going to be a full house for lunch tomorrow,' Robert said. 'You're on reception tomorrow afternoon, I believe.'

'Yes, Bernice has her own luncheon party – at least Mr and Mrs Warburg have – and she is included apparently. It's a family party and I've said she can be off at eleven-thirty. I'm glad to see her getting a break.'

'Nuisance his lordship wanting another night. I told him he would have to change his room. His room has already been booked – the Gladstones.'

'I know.' Grace sounded tired. 'I've been thinking, Robert. Mrs Macready is going to ask us tomorrow about the missing purse, or whatever it is. It is all very well for Alice to say, tell her the facts – she is ninety-nine per cent certain that the young Macready has given it to his lordship.'

'I know, I've been thinking about that. Alice seemed so certain that was the answer, I shall have to suggest it delicately to Mrs M.'

'Rather you than me, you don't believe that, do you?'

'I don't know what to think and it will be an awkward thing to suggest.'

'Come on, let's get to bed, we've had a long day.'

*

Constance lay awake a long time after she had gone to bed: planning what she would do with her last day.

She would shop – no doubt about it, and knew what she would buy. She had made up her mind to buy one of those lovely Chinese bedspreads. All that embroidery, she had never seen anything so pretty in her life. All her mother's linen, which was now hers, of course, was snow white, pristine white, and it took some laundring – not that Constance did it. But for one person, her laundery bill was high. Even the counterpane, or bedspread as they called it nowadays, was white. Crisp and cool in the summer but wouldn't it be a delightful change – that pretty coloured bedspread. She could do with a change after all these years. She just hoped they had one left.

Imagine Sir John meeting up with Joe. But it wasn't all that strange – they belonged to the same associations that still met in the City. So the new woman was not up to much. You couldn't fail to be pleased that you were considered superior. It was human nature.

She would leave early, after breakfast, come back to lunch – then be away. How quickly the time had gone.

Tony Sheridan was not quite sure why he had decided to stay another night. He only knew that if he had left today, he would have felt he missed out on something. The break had not sufficed, he felt he wanted to round it off. Besides, in all truth, he wanted to see Ellis once more. It was kind of unsatisfactory the way it had ended. Anyway, they had managed to find him a room. A different room but just as nice. In the morning he would phone Ellis and suggest a meeting. He hoped she would not be off with her mother to their house near Oxford. Unfinished business, he supposed you could call it, although what the business was, he was not too sure.

The Oxfam charity shop was already open when Dot Turnbull arrived with a great vase of roses.

'Morning, morning,' was said all round and the flowers very much admired.

'Now, I've put a note on the vase – NOT FOR SALE – so watch it. The flowers because it is a special day today. I am going out to lunch, I am being taken *out* to lunch and that doesn't happen very often I can tell you.'

'Where are you going, Mrs Turnbull?'

'To the Old Manor House, no less,' she said smugly.

'Ooh, lovely,' they said.

'I'll leave half an hour early but I am sure you can manage and don't forget to lock up carefully after you.'

They were used to being treated like children and thought nothing of it.

The old man was the first customer, as he frequently was. He came early before the shop was bombarded with women buyers.

'Good morning, Mr Sanderson, lovely day.'

He grunted as he went towards the men's trousers.

'What I thought was,' Tony explained, 'that we could go for a spin – somewhere nice, the Slaughters, perhaps. I haven't been there yet.'

Ellis was pleased but hid her pleasure. 'I thought you were leaving today, in fact, I thought you had gone.'

'Now, I wouldn't leave without saying goodbye, would I?' He sounded reasonable.

'I have no idea what you might do.'

'So, what do you think?'

'What time were you thinking of going?'

'I wasn't, unless you will come with me.'

She felt happier than she had for a long time. 'Ma has gone into Oxford to look at curtain material. Just a moment, I have an idea.'

She thought quickly. 'How would you like to drive me over to our house – Charter Hall?'

Nothing could have pleased Tony more.

'The workmen are off for the weekend, give you a

178

chance to see what they are doing. Perhaps give you some ideas for your own new house.'

'Er, yes, thank you. That would be great. What time shall I pick you up?'

'About eleven? We could perhaps have a snack lunch on the way?'

He found himself looking forward to it.

Constance see off with shopping in mind, and made for the little Oriental shop. Not only did they have the original bedspread, but many others. It was difficult to know which one to choose. And pillow slips, and cushions, what fun it was to be buying for your own home. She had never had time before for replacing worn-out things she had been so busy mending torn linen much as her mother had taught her in days gone by.

There were so many good shops here, with every conceivable thing you might want, and she spent almost until lunch time browsing through them and buying things that took her fancy.

Arriving home laden with parcels, she realised that she had enjoyed her holiday a great deal, it had done her a power of good. She had met different sorts of people, unlike the people she usually mixed with but, even so, she was not sorry to be going home.

She left most of the parcels in the car boot and locked it before making her way back into the hotel where, passing the reception desk, she saw with surprise that Mrs Markham herself was on duty. She looked up with a greeting as Constance came by.

'Oh, Miss Boswell, excuse me, but you have a visitor.'

'A visitor?' Constance's mouth was slightly open and she snapped it shut. She looked around.

'He is waiting on the terrace.'

'He?'

'Yes, he has been here about half an hour.'

'Oh. I've been shopping,' she said. Grace smiled.

179

'Thank you, excuse me,' Constance said, going on to the terrace, but she saw him as clearly as if he had stood up and waved to her. Joe! Her heart began to beat faster. She would know him anywhere: wearing tweeds, reading his newspaper, his short stocky little figure settled in the garden chair, his glasses pushed forward on his nose.

She felt like weeping at the shock of seeing him. She dumped her remaining parcels and stood by his side.

'Joe!'

He stood up immediately and at that, her eyes filled with tears, so pleased did he seem to see her. What a ridiculous situation . . .

'I hope,' he said, 'you can drive me back to London for I came down by train.'

And at the very thought her rather nice eyes glistened. Joe, on a train . . . Oh, it was wonderful to see him. He hadn't changed a bit. The same old Joe but there was no mistaking the expression in his shining dark eyes.

'Sit down,' he said.

'Still giving orders, Joe?' she asked but her voice was a bit shaky.

'Well, someone has to.'

She made herself comfortable and looked at him. Who would have thought . . . 'I suppose Sir John told you I was here.'

'Yes, he is a good friend,' Joe said.

'I thought he was a friend of mine, too,' she said.

'He is,' he said and reached across the table and took her hand. 'Do you want me to leave?'

She shook her head. 'Not after coming all that way by train!' She laughed.

'Oh, well, I have to admit – I've missed you,' he said.

'Are you sure you haven't missed my work?' she said. 'Not dissatisfied with the new lady?'

'Oh, she'll do, for the moment,' he said. 'Can we get a drink here?'

'Of course,' she said. 'The waiter is just inside the door.'

180

He turned towards him and beckoned him over.

'And what will you have?' he asked.

She wasn't a great drinker and he knew that.

'What about champagne?' he asked her, those brown eyes looking into hers.

'Whatever you say, Joe,' she answered.

Who would have thought an hour ago she would be sitting here talking to Joe? But somehow it seemed right.

As they sat drinking champagne, he outlined has plans to her.

'I haven't come down here to bully you,' he said. 'Truly. Truth is I have missed you more than somewhat. Not your work, as you put it, but you, just being there.'

'Well, I've been there a long time, Joe.'

'And to be honest, you shocked me when you said you were going off like that. I really thought we might make a go of it and I was shaken when you turned me down. There, I've said it.'

And that took some doing, as she knew. 'And I've only had a couple of weeks, if that,' she said mildly, 'and perhaps I am thinking of going even farther.'

'Well, if you do, can it be together?'

No one could ask for a nicer proposal, she knew, and she was more than half way to accepting. She had missed him. Spent a lot of time thinking about him.

'I've made plans,' he said. 'I am going to retire.'

'Joe!'

'Yes, I shall be sixty-five in August and, well, the time has come. Time to see what those great sons of mine can do with it.'

'Oh, Joe!' She was astonished to hear his plan.

'Yes, and I thought if we got married, you can live where you like – anywhere – though I'd like to be within driving distance of those grandchildren of mine.'

She looked wistful. 'Yes.'

'And as long as I can play a bit of golf – we'll keep the cottage on at Lymington and buy anywhere you like. We're going to start a new life – how does that sound to you?'

It was a great compliment, she knew. She also knew he didn't relish living out his days on his own any more than she did. And they did have a lot in common.

The two boys as she called them should make a good thing of that business. After all, Joe had kept it going for them, as it had been started by his father for him. A real family firm and much respected in the City.

'Please say you agree, Constance.'

This was pleading indeed from Joe and she knew what her answer would be.

'Well, we can at least give it a try, Joe.'

'Really? Oh, Constance, you've made me really happy,' and he blew his nose loudly.

'Look, after lunch which we'll have here, if that's all right with you, I'll settle the bill and we'll make tracks for home.'

'Your house or mine, Joe?'

'You choose,' he said.

'Yours,' she said. After all, when she got down to it, she could always get rid of that coloured glass.

Putting Charlie on a lead, Genella locked the door of the flat and made her way down to the street. Charlie must have a five-minute walk; he had been cooped up all evening and missed his walk on the green. Charlie looked around in the dark, it was like winter, he thought, for he was an intelligent dog and knew the seasons.

Just to the end of the street, Genella thought. Oh, what tragedies some people made of their lives. Here she was, envying Myra her husband and family, when all the time things were not as they seemed at all.

She felt more sorry for Alan. Taking his children away – he was broken hearted. Surprised too that he and Myra hadn't been happy. She had always thought her sacrifice had been worth it but now she knew that it had been a waste of time. Except of course, that Alan did have two small daughters – she hoped – and wondered at Myra's chances of keeping them.

All that dirty linen to be washed in public. She waited while Charlie stood by the lamp-post, then tugged at the lead to get to the green.

'No, sorry, pet,' she said. 'Tomorrow, we'll go for a nice long walk in the morning.' Even if she opened the shop late.

As for the future, well, they would have to see. There had been a moment or two back there when she had wondered if George, George Turnbull, had any thoughts on their being a twosome. But now that this had cropped up, all thoughts of anything serious would have to be dropped. Strangely enough she had always thought of herself and Alan as a twosome – that her having a shop and him being married to someone else seemed all wrong.

There were a lot of problems to work out and it would all take time. Poor Alan.

'Come on Charlie, home,' she said, and he looked up at her reproachfully.

Chapter Nineteen

The luncheon party was to meet on the terrace for pre-lunch drinks. Carol Warburg was down first, looking resplendent in a flowery dress, her blonde hair cut close to her head, perfectly made up and wearing large sunglasses. Dwight arrive soon afterward – a typical American with his open-necked shirt and green trousers.

Then Bernice came in, escorting Gran, and Carol kissed and hugged her mother, but knew by Bernice's expression that she must not greet her in the same way.

Then George arrived, escorting his mother on one arm and holding Mark's hand with the other. Mark looked up at Bernice and she knew by his look that he wanted her to hold his other hand.

She couldn't recall ever holding a small boy's hand before. And when his little fingers curled round hers, she was thrown into memories of being six years old herself and Gran's hand grasping hers. For no reason at all, she felt close to tears today, which was unusual, because she was not a tearful person; but she was determined to make this Gran's day – a day to remember.

Carol had bought Gran a new dress, gone to Cheltenham with Dwight the day before and, while he was happy to browse around the area, she found what she called 'an older lady's shop', where she would find something suitable for her mother. She decided England was short of these sort of dress shops, it mainly catered for the very young unless you were in a large city, or an expensive area. American stores, she decided, were definitely better for selection. She overlooked the fact that, over the years, she had became distinctly American.

She found what she wanted. A plain light blue skirt and a little jacket sprigged with wild flowers: it would suit the old lady and she would like it. From being quite a well-built woman, her mother had gone down to a size twelve and was shorter than she used to be.

Perhaps not a hat, although women wore them for lunch in the States, but her mother had quite nice hair, a light shade of grey.

It was a special occasion and she hoped it would be remembered as such. She shot a look a Dwight and thought again what a kind man he was to indulge her in this fanciful trip. She wished she had met him years ago but that was the way of life.

When they took their seats, the waiter hovering to see they were settled, she shot a glance at Bernice, wondering what sort of mood she was in. She looked very nice, in brown and beige, which suited her hair colouring, and every now and again she looked down at the small boy as if she was fascinated by him. She hadn't had much to do with small children, thought Carol and wouldn't it be wonderful ... But she was running away with herself – must keep one foot on the ground. After all, it was likely she might never see her mother again and she must make the most of it.

When they were seated, the waiter came with the wine list and Dwight scanned it.

Mark wanted a cold drink and the others wine, so Dwight ordered a bottle of good white to begin with. Gran surprised them all by asking for gin and tonic.

'Gin and tonic!' Carol laughed.

'Yes, why not?' Gran said. 'It's years since I've had one.'

'You may have as many as you like,' Dwight said and leaned towards her with an indulgent smile. 'Ice and lemon?'

'The lot,' Gran said.

Mark was looking around him with interest. He was sitting next to Bernice, which pleased her, and from time to time stole a glance up at her, almost as if he were assessing her.

While Dwight sorted out the order – 'and a whisky sour for me,' Mark tapped Bernice's hand. 'Miss, Bernice, have you got a dog?'

He thought she looked sad. 'No, I haven't,' she said. 'Have you?'

'No, but I hope Daddy will buy us one,' he said, stealing a look at his father, who looked down at him.

'When we're settled, son, after all, you are at school all day, and I am at work. Who would look after him?'

Mark bit his lip and turned back to Bernice. 'You should get a dog,' he said. 'Just a little one, then he wouldn't take up much room.'

'I might do that,' Bernice said. 'it would be company for Gran but she likes birds, you see, and the little dog might frighten them away.'

'Doh!' Mark cried. 'Dogs love birds. It's cats they don't like, isn't it, Dad?'

'What's that, son?'

'Now don't worry your father,' Dot Turnbull said. 'Time enough to get a dog, when you're settled in.'

The thought had struck her for the first time – there was Bernice looking very nice but still with that disapproving look on her face. She supposed it would be permanent by now. But poor lass, it hadn't been easy, and she was wonderful with her Gran. For that she could forgive Bernice anything.

Looking at her son, she thought what a good-looking boy he was. She still called him a boy even though he was approaching middle age. And she supposed Bernice must be the same age since they had gone to school together. For a moment there, she had wondered if Genella and George . . . but it was quiet on that front and she had no idea what was going on. She was anxious for George to marry again – young Mark needed a mother.

And much talking went on around the table until the waiter brought their drinks.

Sipping her gin and tonic, Gran relaxed. She hadn't felt so well for years. Who could have imagined all her family round the same table, to say nothing of Bernice and Carol together.

It was no good wishing, what would be, would be. In her long life, she had come to accept that.

Daydreaming, for she felt a bit woozy, she was so unused to drink, and seeing the three of them Mark, Bernice and George together, it would be easy to imagine them together as a family. But you couldn't order these things. If his heart was taken by the dress-shop lady, well, that was it.

She rose to her feet.

'Thank you, Carol – Dwight – for giving us this lovely day,' she quavered, more than a little unsteady, and sat down abruptly.

Everyone raised their glasses, even young Mark, who copied the grown ups. 'Yes, thank you, Carol, Dwight.' Bernice's throat felt so tight as she held back the tears.

The waiter arrived with the menus, and handed them around, and the discussion as to what they would have seemed to take ages. The menu was so extensive that everyone decided to dispense with a starter in order to make room for a dessert. Dwight took charge and interpreted each order. There was much talk, and George interposed, 'That will be a child's portion for the boy,' while Mark listening, said, 'I could eat a whole one.' 'Yes, but you have to leave room for a pudding, don't you.' And so it went on.

Roast lamb, roast beef, salads, game, salmon, sole – the menu was long and Bernice knew from experience that everything listed would be delicious. Not for nothing was Hobis, the chef, know all over the country as a gourmet's dream. Presently the waiter came to tell them that their table was ready and they joined the other diners in the dining room.

The food was out of this world, and the wine flowed, white wine, red wine. Carol wished this day would go on for ever, and Dwight took photographs, but the luncheon eventually came to an end, with everyone feeling very much better than they had when they arrived.

They took their seats at the large table under the awning and relaxed. The waiter brought coffee and Mark another drink, but it was obvious he was itching to get away and run around.

Her coffee half finished, Bernice stood up and looked down at Mark. 'Shall we go for a walk in the garden?'

His eye shone.

'Excuse us, please,' Bernice said, and George jumped up.

'I'll come with you,' and all the adults round the table smiled.

They wandered off towards the rose garden, which was in full bloom, and sat down on a garden seat, while Mark ran off to explore.

'A very special day,' George said, eyeing Bernice.

She turned to him. 'Yes, you could say that. One I thought could never happen. But imagine Gran's feelings.'

He was silent or a bit 'And yours,' he said at length. Her lip quivered and for a moment he thought she was going to burst into tears.

'George,' she said, 'I wish I didn't fee so – awful towards her, Carol. But I've tried – honestly I have – but it won't go away – the bitterness.'

He began to see how much she had gone through, how it had built up over the years, the feeling of rejection that was so difficult to live with, but it had shaped her into the person she was and all her love had centred on the old lady who had taken her mother's place.

She took off her sunglasses to wipe them and turned to him, and he saw that her lovely green eyes had little flecks in them – full of tears now – possibly the emotions were almost more than she could bear.

He took her hand. 'I expect it cost your mother a great deal to make this journey,' he said and smiled bleakly. 'I don't mean in terms of money.'

'Well, it was about time.'

'But she made it,' George said. 'Isn't that something to be going on with?'

She smiled through the tears. 'But it's all a bit late,' she said.

'Better late than never – at least she made it before—'

'Gran died,' she finished. 'Yes, I'm glad about that. It's just the situation between her and me I can't deal with. Gran is as happy as a sandboy to see her, while I – I didn't want her to come.'

'That's perfectly natural,' George said. 'You were putting off the time when you would come face to face with her.'

'I never wanted to see her again,' Bernice said.

'That's understandable,' George said. 'You felt rejected.'

She took his arm eagerly. 'Yes, that's it. I did. Not wanted. At school I was the only one without a mother.'

Not averse to a bit of self pity, George thought. And yet, it was understandable. And as far as he knew she had no boyfriends to speak of. Shied away. Kept herself to herself. Couldn't relax and expose herself. Vulnerable.

He couldn't remember much about her at school – they had been in the Infants together and he had played mostly with boys, while she, Bernice, had been inclined to lag behind the other girls – not join in.

He decided to take the plunge. It was now or never. 'This will be the start of a new era for you, I hope,' he said. 'Everything has changed. And it has been a super day, hasn't it?'

189

She smiled, and when she smiled, her face was transformed. He would tell her so. 'You look so different when you smile. Very pretty.'

'And you are a nice man, George,' she said. 'It's not been easy for you, either, has it?'

'No,' he said shortly, and she wondered how much he had loved his wife. She must have been about thirty something when she died. Sue – that was her name. How awful – and she thought she was hard done by. Mark came running towards them. 'There's a little river, a stream, just over there,' he said. 'I think there could be fish in it.'

'Do you fish?' Bernice asked George.

'No, but I have a feeling I will in the future,' he grinned.

'Well, let's walk back.' And he took Mark's hand as they began the stroll back.

'You know, if ever you need a babysitter, I'll gladly oblige. I think he's cute – an interesting little boy.'

'I have a better idea,' George said. 'Why don't you and I go out one evening – cinema, dinner – or dinner at the cottage. I'm quite a good cook.'

'Oh, I didn't mean—' Bernice said, her face flushing.

'You underestimate your charms,' George said smoothly. 'How about it?' And she actually smiled at him.

'That would be nice,' she said. 'I will look forward to that.'

When they returned to the table, coffee had been served but the waiter brought fresh.

'How are you, Gran?' George asked.

'Having a whale of a time,' she said, and smiled across at Carol.

Carol got up and brushed down her skirt.

'I must take a turn round this lovely garden before I go,' she said. 'It is so beautiful. Coming with me, Bernice?'

Startled, Bernice hesitated, then pushed back her chair. She could hardly refuse.

'Yes,' she said, and the two walked off together.

What wouldn't I give to hear that conversation, Dot Turnbull thought.

But Gran was dozing slightly, almost as if she hadn't realised what was going on.

They walked towards the rose gardens, saying nothing, until they came to the area where beds of petunias and geraniums, lobelias and busy lizzies held up their faces in the sun. There was a trellis walk, where ramblers and clematis intertwined, it was altogether a blissful spot.

Carol patted a seat.

'Let's sit down for a moment, shall we?' she asked, taking off her sunglasses.

She didn't look the same woman without them and Bernice sat down without a word.

'I know,' Carol began. 'That you will never forgive me—'

'That's not the right word,' Bernice said, but her shoulders were stiff and she was in no way relaxed.

'I would just like to tell you something before I leave,' Carol said. 'You may not want to hear it, but I shall tell you anyway. It makes no difference to our relationship – that is for you to decide.'

Still Bernice said nothing.

'I went, as you know to South Carolina,' she said. 'To find my father. I can't explain it – it was something I had to do.'

Bernice waited.

'I found him,' she said bleakly and at this Bernice looked straight at her.

'You found him? But I thought—'

'I know you did.'

'The Army authorities found his address for me and sure enough it was in South Carolina. The only thing was he was not killed in France – he was married, with a family of three sons.'

Bernice gasped. 'No!'

'I put up at a nearby hotel, well, B and B to be precise,

191

for I had no money, and I watched that farm where he lived for a week. In a nutshell, I discovered that he had been engaged when he met Mum. But, of course, she was ignorant of that. He went to France, leaving her pregnant – with me – and when she didn't hear, she presumed he had been killed in action, for she had no rights as his girlfriend and no one would have notified her as to what happened to him. She quite naturally assumed he had been killed in action, which was the last letter she had from him, that he was in northern France.'

The tears were now running down Bernice's face.

'I hung about that farm for a week – until I saw him. He was standing outside the wide gates with two men – he was in the middle and I knew him straightaway from a photo Mum kept on her dressing table. I did that three times, before I accepted the fact that I was on a wild-goose chase – and I would never be able to tell Mum about it.'

Bernice was crying now and it was as if all the pent-up emotion over the years was released.

'I couldn't come back – I couldn't – Mum and I were very close. After all, I had entrusted you to her but I never expected to find that. I thought and thought about it, but I kept telling myself – not yet – not yet – I couldn't face her – and I couldn't lie. That's how it was. It may sound a weak excuse to you, but it was very real to me. She adored him, idolised him.'

Bernice dried her eyes and put her sunglasses on.

'Not much of an excuse, is it?'

But Bernice just put out her hand and covered Carol's for a brief moment. 'Thank you for telling me.'

They walked back together across the rose garden and the lawn to where the others sat waiting, anxiously – wondering.

But nothing was said and Bernice was unusually quiet.

As it got towards tea time, everyone went back to Gran's tiny cottage, Gran to go upstairs for a bit of a nap, while the others sat in the small garden.

'I shall miss this,' Carol said.

'We will come again,' Dwight said.

'I hope you will come and see my small house in Akers Green,' George said.

'And I have to thank you for all your mother does for Gran – she's been a real friend,' Carol said. 'Oh, here they are.'

'They are very fond of each other,' George said. 'Keep each other going.'

'Well, it was your old gran who started it off, wasn't it? I remember her.'

'Yes, true,' George said.

'Anyone for a cup of tea?' Bernice said, and smiled.

What a difference, George thought. I wonder what Carol said to her. She looks relaxed – almost happy.

And Bernice was . . .

'Come and help me with the tea things,' Bernice said to Carol, leading the way back into the kitchen.

A little startled, but pleased, Carol went over to the dresser while Bernice put the kettle on, then turned to face her mother.

'So many wasted years,' she said sadly. 'And it's my fault – I never looked at it from your point of view.'

'Mine too,' Carol said and smiled wryly. 'What people do to each other.'

Bernice kissed her mother swiftly, so unused was she to showing her feelings, but Carol felt a warm glow inside her. 'And you've looked after Gran so well.'

The kettle boiled and Bernice made the tea.

'We shall come again next year,' Carol said. 'Now that we've discovered each other, we must keep in touch.' Bernice felt that a great weight had been lifted from her shoulders.

They carried the tea things into the small paved garden and George looked up seeing the different expression on Bernice's face. Something was said out there, he thought,

Bernice looks relaxed, pretty, and suddenly he remembered her as a small girl at school with two long plaits and laughing green eyes ...

At his side Mark was pulling his arm. 'Dad, could Bernice come with us on to the green this evening. She likes dogs, she told me – and perhaps we could—'

George's eyes twinkled.

'Yes, I should think so,' he said. 'We'll ask her.'

Chapter Twenty

Ellis Macready was waiting in the lounge when Tony came out of the lift. It had rained slightly during the night and he saw that she carried a rainproof jacket and wore jeans and a jersey. Her hair was pulled back off her face and she wore no make up – indeed she was at her plainest. She looked about sixteen.

But that was Ellis and he was pleased that he had booked in for another day. Also delighted he was going at last to see Charter Hall, having heard so much about it. He was curious, to say the least. Also, he was determined to give back the tiepin to Ellis – for once in his life, he would do the right thing. He had thought about it; but she was obviously a generous-minded girl and on impulse had wanted him to have it.

'Ellis.' She looked up and smiled – a rare event. She too, then, must be looking forward to the trip.

'I'll get the car and bring it round.'

'I'll come with you,' she said, jumping up.

Now the sun was shining and it promised to be a warm day. The flower beds had received the rain gratefully and the raindrops glistened like pearls in the artemisia mollis.

'Well,' he said, when they were seated. 'You must show me the way.'

'Make for Oxford,' she said. 'I'll tell you where to turn off.'

They drove through the village and out the other side.

'How is your mother? Bearing up?'

'Yes, – and no. The past few days she seems to have something on her mind and I keep asking her but she says it's nothing.'

'You know, having a large house done over with so many alterations is a bit of a problem.'

'You'd know, would you?' Ellis bantered.

'No, but I can imagine,' he said. 'Left here?'

'Yes, then farther on you'll see the signpost to Stanfield, turn left again there.'

They drove in silence for a few minutes. 'So, you've finished looking at houses then?' Ellie said.

'Yes, for the moment, I've seen some, learned a lot.'

'Have you?'

'Thanks to you,' he grinned. 'But I'll shelve it, I think for the time being.'

'Would you look somewhere else? After all, the counties do vary.'

'No, I fancy the Cotswolds but it covers quite a large area.'

They were on a wide lane with no other traffic about when out of a small intersection a cyclist appeared without making any effort to stop. Tony jammed on the brakes hard, Ellis gave a little cry and hid her face. Looking out, Tony was in time to see the cyclist give a jaunty wave. They sat huddled, shocked ...

'Christ!' Tony said when he got his breath back. 'Are you all right?'

Ellie was shaking and had gone very pale.

'I'm sorry.'

'It wasn't your fault,' she said. 'How can people do that?'

She looked up at him, and suddenly, his arms were round her, holding her tight. 'Ellie, Ellie, it's a good job you had your seat belt on you might have been killed.' Then he realised the enormity of what he was saying.

196

'You, too,' she said, with a weak grin.

'Let's pull over,' he said. He eased the car over to the edge of the field where it bumped a bit then came to a standstill.

He was aware of an emotion that he had never yet encountered. A feeling for someone other than himself. This little thing at his side – no tears, – screams – it had been horrifying while it lasted, only a matter of moments.

He tilted her face. 'Are you sure you are all right? I know it was a shock. Would you like to get out of the car?'

'No, I'd rather stay with you, I'd feel safer,' and she smiled a tremulous smile.

They looked into each other's eyes for what seemed a full minute, then slowly Tony's lips met hers, full and sweet, and her arms went around his neck, holding him ever closer as if she would never let him go. Her lips, beneath his, parted and he thought he had never known such bliss. A mad thought went through his head – was this what Johnnie had – and let go – before putting Johnnie at the back of his mind for ever and releasing Ellis, whose eyes were wide with wonder. Her eyes were beautiful – why had he never noticed them before? In fact, she herself was beautiful. The most beautiful woman he had ever seen. There had been girls, lots of them, but never a girl like this one. The thought crossed his mind that this was why he had been so loath to get home. Fate had predicted otherwise.

'I've always liked cyclists,' he said at length.

'Me, too,' Ellis said.

They stayed in the car for what seemed an eternity, reluctant to change this spot for anywhere else.

At length, Tony suggested that they stop for lunch before arriving at Charter Hall. They stopped at The Bricklayers' Arms on the way.

'Not a very romantic name for a pub,' he said to Ellis as, hand in hand, they walked inside.

'It's pretty though,' Ellis said. 'Shall we sit in the

197

garden? There is no one about, so quiet.'

The place was almost deserted at almost midday. The bartender came out to them.

'Can I help you, sir? There's good food at the bar.'

'Yes, we'll see to that later, but I suggest a bottle of champagne.'

'Tony! You're driving,' Ellis said.

'Oh, yes, sorry. Well, what shall it be? How far are we away from your home?'

'Oh, about ten miles.'

'Then we'll have two glasses of your best red, and order later.' He had never felt more relaxed and happy.

When the bartender brought the wine and the menu, which was simple enough, they ordered, then Tony looked at Ellis whose eyes were sparkling.

His mind was such a maelstrom of thoughts that he couldn't think clearly. Sitting opposite him was the girl he had fallen in love with. He knew that without any shadow of a doubt. He had never before felt like this about any woman. Was he mad? What did they have in common? And yet . . . She wasn't the sort of girl you could entice into an affair. And he wasn't sure that's what he wanted. He also knew that he could be impulsive and regret things afterwards. But this feeling was not like that. He was sure. Not only did she attract him physically but they got on so well. And they had nothing in common – or had they? He was at his ease with her – and he wanted her.

All through the meal he sat with a sense of wonder, while Ellis sat relaxed, as if she read his thoughts and the doubts that accompanied them.

This wasn't the time, he thought, knowing he was on the verge of proposing. He was relieved when the waiter arrived with their meal.

Several times they caught each other's eyes, unwilling to believe what had come to pass. Once, he covered her hand with his, and smiled.

They were both playing for time . . .

To say Tony was surprised at his first sight of the Hall was an understatement.

Beating anything he had seen yet, it stood in extensive grounds which disappeared into the distance. Great iron gates were open now, a long drive leading up to the house, an iron balustrade, at the centre of which were two large stone creatures, dogs or lions, Tony was not sure which.

At the top of the steps Ellis rang the bell, and the house-keeper came to the door, accompanied by two enormous dogs, who barked and jumped up at Ellis until she told them to behave, and sit quietly.

'Hello, Mrs Banks. Is Mother at home?' she asked, leading Tony into the magnificent hall.

'No Ellis, she's not back from Oxford yet but she phoned to say she won't be long.'

'And the workmen gone?'

'For the weekend.' The housekeeper looked hard at Tony.

'This is Mr Sheridan, Annie, a friend of ours.'

'How do you do,' Annie said.

Tony thought he must be dreaming.

Ellis took his hand. 'Come on, I'll show you around.'

Walking through the hall to the drawing room, and the newly half built conservatory, he could quite see what an advantage the new extension would be. Scaffolding was everywhere, builders' skips, cement mixers – while outside the fields seemed to go on for miles.

'How much land do you have here?' he asked.

'Almost seventy acres,' she said.

'Whew!' he said. 'And what do you do with it?'

'Farming, we have an estate manager. A couple of horses, oh, I didn't ask you if you ride?'

'Well,' he said. 'I used to.'

'We've just two horses now.'

'What do you grow in the garden?'

'Vegetables, a little corn. I'm trying to create a flower garden – a real garden. Come and see. I'd like it to look like the garden at The Old Manor House.'

She led him down the steps to a larger area, which had been planted with new trees, and a lawn, and flower beds.

'What a splendid idea. How could you bear to leave it, and go to the hotel?'

'It was mother's idea to go to The Old Manor House. She wanted to be out the way of the workmen.'

She took his hand. 'Come and see over the house.'

She showed him the downstairs part of the house. It was old, seventeenth century, but a great deal of money had been spent on it.

'No wonder you know a lot about houses,' he said.

'I've grown up with this one,' she said. 'Since we left the USA we practically live here. We both love it and Father left it in our care. He loved it. When he died we vowed to care for it, and improve it – and that's what we do, mainly. It's hard work.'

It was so much grander what he had imagined that Tony was unable to take the situation in.

Upstairs, the bedrooms and guest rooms were exquisitely furnished – a touch of Mrs Macready here, he thought. Her taste throughout was apparent.

Ellis glanced at him. 'Yes, you are right. 'It's mother's taste, which I haven't inherited, it seems. Still, when you know what you want and there are excellent workmen to be found, you can manage it.'

And for a moment, he remembered his two acquaintances, without whom he would never be here. Their talk of jewels and riches and wealth and he found himself feeling distinctly uneasy. Would she want to marry him if she knew the kind of man he was?

For he couldn't have managed things better if he had planned it: to fall in love – at forty – and this was before he knew the set up.

But there had been – and was – something about Ellis

that touched his heart. There was no question in his mind that she was the woman for him – with or without her wealth. And the tiepin. . .

'Ellie, ' he said. 'Just one thing,' and withdrew from his top pocket the tiny packet.

'I would like you to take this back – it was so generous of you – but I didn't deserve it.'

'You don't like it?' she was shocked.

'Of course I like it but – you are too generous, you shouldn't have given it to me. I know it's worth a lot of money.'

'Well, good,' she said.

Somehow he was going to have to tell her that he wasn't quite what he seemed.

'Let's have some tea,' she suggested, and went into the kitchen to ask for it to be brought outside.

When it arrived they sat to enjoy the view and to ponder over the last few hours.

'Ellis,' Tony said seriously. 'You don't know a lot about me – about my life, my background.'

'And you don't know a lot about me,' she said quietly.

'But I can see your background from here, while—'

'What do you really do?' she said.

'This and that,' he said. 'I'm an odd bod, like you.'

'What's that – an odd bod?'

'I suppose it means an odd body, different, not like other people – and you are the same.'

'Oh, I like that,' she said. 'An odd bod. Yes, that's what I am. But you were telling me about what you do.'

'I've never really settled,' he said. 'I've done lots of things, tried lots of things – acting, art, antiques, bit of banking work for my father – that was a dead loss – one thing and another – I don't have a profession, I am a no-account person,' he said.

'You're not a no-account person,' she assured him. 'An odd bod, yes, but you will turn out to be somebody, you'll see.'

'You reckon?' God, what faith she had in him. Perhaps if his family had had as much faith. . .

'Now, it's my turn,' she said, and faced him squarely.

'What you don't know about me, is that I am not Mrs Macready's daughter.'

And at this he was stunned. 'What do you mean?'

'I am the daughter of her brother, Lionel Masters and a Sarah Jane Masters, who both died in a car accident, leaving me to the care of my aunt, Mary-Ann Macready. I am penniless, apart from what my aunt gives me, which will tell you why I stay. But that's not the only reason. She is not a well woman, she has a weak heart and I look after her. She is kindness itself to me – they both were – but rich daughter, I am not. I have an allowance which I like to think I earn.' And for a moment she looked scared as to what he might say.

Tony got up and came round the table, taking her in his arms and kissing her. Again he thought he must be dreaming.

'Oh, you are nice,' she said, wiping her eyes.

'I went to live with them when I was twelve years old, and they treated me like their own daughter. My uncle he left me jewels – one of which you have – and he adored me anyway.'

Tony kissed her eyes.

'You were quite right,' she went on, 'we are a couple of odd bods, not quite what we seem.'

'There is just one more thing,' he said. 'Um, perhaps I should tell you now, my father is Lord Redingham, and I am the black sheep, the failure.'

She laughed out loud. 'Oh, Tony! You've got to be joking. Wait until Ma hears.'

There was the sound of a car coming down the drive and, looking up, they saw Mrs Macready getting out and coming towards them.

'Well, this is a surprise!' she exclaimed. 'Nice to see you Tony.'

202

'Did you have a good day?' Ellis asked, going forward to take her shopping bags.

'Yes, very satisfactory, and you, what do you think of the house, Tony? Am I doing the right thing?'

'I should say so, Mrs Macready,' Tony said. 'It is going to be wonderful.'

Mrs Macready looked from one to the other of them. 'Yes, well, I think a drink is called for,' she said. 'Let me get rid of these parcels and I'll join you. Oh, it was so warm in Oxford and everywhere was packed.'

She disappeared into the house and Tony and Ellis exchanged a swift kiss.

That night, back at The Old Manor House, after they had got ready for bed, Ellis decided that the time had come to be frank about the tiepin.

'Ma, Ma, you remember it was Tony's birthday a few days ago?'

'Yes, dear.'

'You know the tiepin Dad left me?' Mrs Macready swung round, 'Yes, what?'

'Well I gave it to Tony for his birthday.'

'You what? Oh, you naughty girl! I thought it had been stolen!'

'But it was mine, wasn't it? Mine to give?'

'Yes, of course, my dear, but you should have said. I have been so worried and daren't tell you. I thought you would be heartbroken and so upset.'

'I'm sorry Ma, I didn't think you'd notice it and that you might be cross at my giving it to Tony.'

'My dear, I am delighted. I daren't tell you in case you would be upset. I know how fond you were of your father – that's what's been worrying me.'

'Oh, I'm sorry.'

'Never mind. No problem, dear,' she said, dreading having to tell that nice hotel man what had really happened.

*

Tony Sheridan was talking urgently to the nice hotel man, Robert Markham. 'I would be really grateful, if you could manage it,' he said.

Robert perused the ledgers. 'I am awfully sorry but we are fully booked.'

'No, I wanted tonight,' Tony said, looking as disappointed as only he knew how.

'Seen something you like, sir?' Robert asked.

'Er, yes, you could say that,' Tony murmured.

'There is just one possibility,' Robert said doubtfully, 'we keep a small spare room, it really is not part of the hotel, a private room we use for our own—'

'That would be fine,' Tony pounced on it at once. 'Could I take it – is that—'

'Well, if you are agreeable. It is not of the standard of the room that you have.'

'No problem,' Tony beamed. 'I'll book it if I may.'

He had some urgent business to see to.

Chapter Twenty-one

On Sunday morning, Mrs Macready was downstairs in reception first thing.

'Good morning, Mrs Macready. How can I help you?'

'I would like to see Mr Markham.'

'I'm not sure if he is available.' Bernice was not sure also that he would appreciate being troubled on his late morning.

'It is a matter of some urgency,' Mrs Macready said.

'Very well, I'll see what I can do, if you would like to take a seat, Mrs Macready,' Bernice said.

Five minutes later, Robert appeared, suave as ever, with a warm greeting. 'You wished to see me, Mrs Macready?'

She looked around. 'Could we—'

'Of course,' he said and led the way to his inner sanctum.

He offered her a seat and sat opposite her.

'I have come to apologise,' Mrs Macready said. He raised his brows.

'About the missing piece of jewellry,' she said and he gave an inward sigh of relief, and waited.

'It has been found,' she said. 'My daughter had given the piece to Mr Sheridan – for his birthday, as a secret – a secret I knew nothing about,' and she laughed apologetically. 'I am so sorry.'

'I see.'

He wasn't going to let her off so easily. 'And she didn't tell you?'

'No, well you know what the young are. I expect she thought I wouldn't notice its absence, but of course I did. I know every piece of jewellery in that box.'

He stood up. 'Well, I am very glad it has been found and the mystery solved. I had no worries on that score, since I know my system is sound. But it is a problem when that kind of thing happens and we don't like our guests to be disturbed.'

She was delighted to have got it over with – such a nice man.

'Thank you for letting me know,' he said opening the door for her and doing his best not to hurry along to give Grace the news.

Grace had just come out of the bathroom and was doing her hair. 'What was it?'

He closed the door behind him. 'You'll never guess!'

'So tell me.'

'That was Mrs Macready, come to apologise. The missing piece of jewellery has been found.'

She swivelled in her chair.

'Well, Alice was right. Young Macready had given it to Sheridan as a birthday present.'

'No!'

'So Alice was right.'

'Alice is always right.' And they laughed together.

Robert Markham was on the phone.

'Alice? Everything all right?'

'Yes, Dad. OK with you?'

'Just thought I'd let you know that all's well on the tiepin front.'

She laughed. 'Been found has it?'

'You were right – young Macready had given it to Sheridan for a birthday present.'

'Didn't I say? Trust Alice.' She smiled to herself.

206

'Thanks for letting me know, Dad.'

It was a fine Sunday morning and Genella Hastings decided that she would take Charlie for a short walk before Alan arrived.

He had telephoned the night before, sounding very distressed and invited himself round for Sunday – lunch – or whatever Genella wanted.

'Of course, Alan,' she said. 'Anything you like.'

She knew he wanted to talk and she had cold roast chicken in the fridge and plenty of salad and French bread.

Her heart went out to him. Things had gone from bad to worse, according to his telephone calls, and she would wait to see what today brought.

There were few people about on this early morning and Charlie ran around to his heart's delight, dashing for the ball that Genella repeatedly threw to him.

Slowly, they walked home, and once indoors, Genella dried his paws, saw that he had fresh drinking water, made herself fresh coffee and awaited Alan's arrival.

She did not have long to wait. When the doorbell rang, she pressed the button and up the stairs came Alan, pale faced and looking drained. He put his arms around her, mainly to comfort himself, and she held him.

It seemed a natural thing to do, to comfort him. After all, that had been together a long time before tragedy struck and drove them apart.

She put on a bright face 'Coffee?' she said. 'You are just in time.'

When she gave him the cup he put it on the table in front of him.

'Oh, Alan! You look so miserable,' she said. 'But I do understand.'

'It's the girls. They are so upset, they know something is up even though we don't discuss anything between us in front of them.'

'They are old enough to understand something is going

207

on, especially Susie, what is she – seven?'

He nodded. He felt like weeping. 'And Rosie five.'

'It's awful when a marriage breaks up – for everyone. Now drink this and tell me what's happened.'

She sat listening, while he told her that that were going to divorce as soon as possible. They had both agreed. Perfectly amicably – at least on Myra's side.

'They've gone to live at Simpson's place – that's his name – at least he has a house they can live in – and she of course seems quite excited at the prospect.' This seemed to upset him more than somewhat.

'We've decided between ourselves – of course, it all has to be finalised by the solicitors – that I will have the children every other weekend and access when I like.'

'Oh, that's great,' Genella said. 'Aren't you pleased with that?'

'Are you joking? I don't what to lose them at all.'

She went to sit beside him on the sofa and took his hand. 'Is there really no hope of getting back together?'

'No, she's carrying his child, remember?'

'Of course I do.'

'And she has this bee in her bonnet that we never should have married, that I never loved her.'

'But you did, didn't you?' she pressed him.

Never as much as I loved you, he wanted to say, but it was unfair to implicate her – it was not her fault they had done what they did.

'Well,' she said brightly now. 'What are you going to do?'

Again, he wanted to say – come back to you. There is nothing in the world I want more.

'How do you feel about my bringing the children sometimes when I come to see you?'

'Oh, Alan!' and her eyes filled with tears. 'Of course you may bring them, anytime you like.'

She had given the matter quite a lot of thought when she could see which way the wind was blowing. And she had decided that, as she had always wanted children until fate decreed otherwise she must play it very carefully. They would get back together, of course they would, and nothing would please her more. But another woman's children? They were Alan's as well and she still loved Alan more than any man she had ever met.

There was lots of sorting out to do but first she must meet these little girls – Alan's daughters. Myra had sounded quite reasonable about it, after all. But she was having another child. Lucky woman, Genella thought, just a little bitterly – but out of this I get Alan back.

Mrs Macready was going over to Charter Hall on this fine Sunday morning when Ellis announced that she was going to church.

'Oh,' her mother hesitated. 'I would rather like to come with you but I—'

'I'll go and tell you what the service is like,' Ellis said, for she hoped to see something of Tony.

'Very well, dear, I shall be back in time for lunch.' And with that she went to the car park to pick up the car.

Ellis made her way back to their room and had just closed the door, when her telephone bleeped.

'Ellie,' and her heart leapt. It was Tony, just as she had hoped. She had missed him at breakfast not knowing that he was changing his room for another.

'Tony, where are you?'

'In the foyer, what are you doing today?'

'Just going to church,' she said. 'St Rupert's. Have you ever been?'

'To church, yes. To St Rupert's, I am afraid not.'

'Like to join me?' she asked.

At the sound of her voice he was overjoyed. 'Why not?'

'Meet me here in twenty minutes,' she said, 'and we'll go together.'

Eyeing himself in the mirror, he smiled to himself. What a turn up for the book. Tony Sheridan going to church –

209

wouldn't his mother be pleased.

His heart leapt at the sight of Ellis, soberly dressed in a dark skirt and white jacket, and he kissed her briefly and took her arm.

'Aren't you afraid someone will see us?' she said, as they walked across the greensward towards the church.

'I hope they do,' he said, 'then there will be no mistakeing us as a couple.'

Ellis took a deep breath. This was the happiest moment in her life.

The church was so pretty inside and there were quite a few people there that Ellis recognised by sight.

The stained-glass windows were beautiful and she was reminded of a church back home which she and her mother attended sometimes. They were not regular churchgoers. In the Episcopalian church everyone greeted each other, holding hands with the person next to them, but this was more formal, really old English, which charmed her; her mother would love it.

The small choir sang, then the congregation, and the vicar spoke from the pulpit which turned out to be a lesson for peace and more kindness throughout the world. Then more hyms and Ellis noticed that Tony joined in wholeheartedly and knew all the words of the hymns, some of which were new to her.

From time to time she stole a sidelong glance at him unable to believe she had fallen in love with this exraordinary – odd bod – and who, if she were to believe her instincts, felt the same way about her.

They all rose to their feet for the final hymn, the collection plate came round and soon it was over.

The vicar stood at the door and shook hands with them and together they made for the avenue of cypress trees that fringed the church. There were seats here and there but most people seemed anxious to get home to Sunday lunch.

Holding her hand Tony led her to the last seat almost enveloped by overgrown cypresses. He dusted it with a snow-white handkerchief and bade her sit down.

'Why St Rupert's, I wonder?' Ellis asked.

'Someone's patron saint, I daresay say,' said Tony. 'Where is your mother this morning?'

'Gone to Charter Hall, she'll be back for lunch.'

'Oh, then we'll join her. In the meantime, I have something to ask you.'

She turned startled eyes to his.

'I can't kneel down,' he said, 'the ground is damp – but Ellie, my darling – will you marry me?'

'Will I what?' Her mouth was open.

'Will you marry me – please?'

'Oh, Tony!'

She hugged him. 'Of course I will, of course I will!' And they kissed, surprising no one who might be passing who had seen all this sort of thing before.

'You mean it?' she asked him, looking straight into his eyes.

'Of course I do!'

Together, hand in hand, they walked back to the hotel, and sat in the garden, deep in thought, both of them imagining that this was some kind of dream.

Emerging from the hotel, Mrs Macready looked around for them. A warm glow filled her heart as she saw them, hands locked together on a seat in the garden.

'Oh, there you are! Were you waiting for me?'

They smiled at her. Their faces glowed as she sat down besides them.

'Mom,' Ellis said quietly. 'We have some news for you.'

'News? What sort of news? Is something wrong?'

'Tony and I are engaged,' Ellis said, smiling into his eyes, but seeing the joy on her mother's face.

'Wonderful! When did this happen?'

'Today,' Ellis said. 'After Church. I know it's sudden but ...'

Mary-Ann took a deep breath 'That's wonderful!' she said and kissed Ellis and took Tony's hand in hers.

'Congratulations,' she said. 'I am delighted.'

'Oh, and something else,' Ellis said, casually. 'Tony's father is Lord Redingham—'

But Mrs Macready had fainted.

'Don't worry,' Ellis said jumping to her feet. 'She often does. . .

Chapter Twenty-two

It was a year later, a fine June morning, and Grace had just got back from the hairdresser.

'She seems to be settling in all right,' she said to Robert, having just passed through reception. She was referring to the new receptionist, Joanna Wilding, who had been there for just two weeks.

'Yes nice girl, very efficient, and the clients like her. What more can we want?'

'We are going to miss Bernice. She was here when we came.'

'Yes, but I'm pleased about the wedding. A busy day today, Robert. Oh, but I do love a wedding, and a local one, I'd better go up and change – it's some time since we actually attended a wedding.'

'Yes, and never one in this church,' Robert said.

'I still can't get over that, the Warburgs, I mean, Mrs Warburg being Bernice's mother. Talk about truth being stranger than fiction.'

'Come on then, we've a lot to do.'

There was an enormous vase of madonna lilies in the window of the charity shop and several bowls of flowers. It looked very festive and the women were really having a nice day. Dot had supplied them with a bottle of champagne to drink the couple's health, for her son was getting married today, to a girl he had gone to school with, she said, the receptionist at the The Old Manor House.

'When shall we open the champagne?' asked Liz.

'After they are married, about one-thirty I should think,' said Sandra, who was in charge.

What a lovely day for a wedding.

Susie Bembridge and her sister Rosie were hopping around the little house on the green in a state of great excitement.

'Can we really go to see the wedding, Genella? You promised.'

Genella smiled at them, fixing her hat and looking in the mirror. 'Of course, I said so. Now get your things, Rosie, and we'll make our way.'

They were not guests but she had promised the children that they would see the wedding of Bernice Holden and George Turnbull this Saturday at St Rupert's Church. Everyone was going, everyone in the village, that is, for the Turnbulls and the Holdens were old residents.

Three months previously, Alan Bembridge's divorce had come through and he had bought the small cottage on the green, deeming it a good and convenient place to live for when his daughters came to stay. His previous house had been sold and the money divided between him and his ex-wife, Myra. In a few weeks he and Genella would marry; it would be a quiet wedding, their second and she would move into the cottage. It was so much more convenient for two small girls and they all loved it.

Genella was in her element, these two little girls were a delight to her, and she adored them. Both like Alan, she hardly ever thought of the fact that they belonged to Myra as well, and enjoyed the weekends and odd times that they came home. Alan lived with her now, prior to their wedding, for four months previously his ex-wife had given birth to a son – her lover's child.

It was the end of an era, they told themselves, and looked

214

forward to being officially married in September.

On their second visit to The Old Manor House, Carol and Dwight were getting ready for the wedding, for Dwight was to give Bernice away in the absence of ther real father.

Carol again looked resplendent, her hair even more blonde beneath her large elegant hat, her outfit, which she had brought with her specially chosen in New York. But she was more concerned that Dwight would look the part.

'I can't believe this is happening,' she said. 'And George is such a darling. I couldn't have wished for a better husband for her.'

'She has changed a great deal since we last saw her,' Dwight said. 'She is positively radiant, looks more like you,' he said, for he adored her.

'Oh, get away with you,' laughed Carol. 'Now I'm going over the road to see how Mum is getting on, although with Dot to help her she is bound to have found something nice.'

Her mother was in a state of high excitement and she looked wonderful for her age. She and Dot had shopped and both bought outfits on Dot's advice, for if there was anything Dot knew about, it was clothes.

'Oh, Mum, you look wonderful, and so do you, Dot!' She kissed her mother, who was wearing a navy two piece and a large cream hat, festooned with a veil and flowers.

'What do you think?' Dot asked anxiously.

'Fabulous!' Carol said. 'I love the hat, Mum, you look great.'

She took Dot to one side. 'Do you think she will be all right?' she asked. 'It's a lot of excitement for one day.'

'Good Lord, yes!' Dot said. 'She's having a whale of a time and you look smashing, too,' she said to Carol.

'Well,' and Carol sighed. 'It's a fantastic day, isn't it?' She wiped away a tear, a tear of happiness. 'Soon be time,' she said, looking at her watch.

*

215

Mr and Mrs Joseph Maxwell were sitting in the lounge of The Old Manor House celebrating the date that Joe had arrived and proposed yet again and Constance had accepted him.

'I expect the wedding party will be arriving soon,' Constance said. 'Isn't it exciting for them?'

'Who is it?' Joe asked, not much interested.

'The receptionist girl, apparently she has been here years, and she was here when I came last year. She is marrying a local man and the reception is here. I love this hotel, Joe.'

'Yes, very nice,' he said, 'excellent.' He put his hand over hers. 'It did occur to me, Constance, that perhaps you would like to move here – to the Cotswolds, I mean.'

He was furious that they had wasted so much time and he was happier than he had ever been. 'I know we looked at different places and there is no need to be in London now.'

'But we have the cottage at Lymington and your little boat,' she smiled indulgently.

She had had no idea she could be so happy. They had been married for six months and she could still not get used to the idea.

'No, I'll keep that going,' he said, 'but instead of a London flat, as you suggested, what about a cottage here? It's a lovely little place.'

Her mind harked back to when she had gone to the estate agent to inquire about the cottage on the green. 'Well, I don't know Joe,' she said doubtfully. 'I love it here but let's just keep it for visits. There is nowhere nicer.' She smiled, her blue eyes shining into his.

'Ah, I can hear something,' and she turned in time to see the bride arriving at the hotel entrance.

The Honourable Ellis Sheridan and her husband Tony were spending the weekend with her mother at Charter Hall. They had been married for nine months, and neither of them could believe they could ever have been so happy.

'Tony, I have an idea, why don't we pop over to The Old Manor House for a drink? I have an idea the receptionist there is geting married today,' she looked at him pleadingly. 'Could we?'

'Darling, do you really want to?'

'Yes, I do, to please me?'

'Well, of course, if you're sure you want to.'

She huried into the house to tell her mother and he watched her go. His beloved Ellis, with little rounded tum. He couldn't believe it – five months' pregnant, he was to be a father...

There was a crowd waiting outside the church; the path to the door was crowded with loyal sightseers, neighours and local residents, and Alan and Genella, each holding the hand of a little girl tightly, watched as the beautiful bride emerged from the church, her groom at her side. Behind came a small boy, faultlessly dressed, looking as pleased as punch. There followed Granny Holden and Dot Turnbull, but all eyes were on the bride, who looked radiant.

In cream silk, her dress simple with long tight sleeves, and a flowing lace veil held in place by a small posy of pink rosebuds, her husband glanced at her ... his beautiful bride.

She looked up at him with those lovely green eyes, brimming over now with happiness as he reached over to kiss her ...

217

Apple Tree Cottage
Rose Boucheron

Ruth Durling and her husband, John, had always dreamed of retiring to a little cottage in the Cotswolds. However John had died before they had ever realised that dream. Now, eight months after his death and with their children all grown up and raising families of their own, Ruth has taken the decision to move to the country by herself.

Apple Tree Cottage, in the village of Little Astons, seems perfect for her needs. Ruth falls in love with the house the moment she sets eyes on it. But village life is far different to living in Cheltenham and Ruth is still finding it hard adjusting to life without her beloved husband. However as Ruth begins to settle in to her new home, slowly she begins to make friends and discovers that Little Astons has its secrets ...